MURDERED BY CROWS

Reuben Cole Westerns Book 5

STUART G. YATES

This for everyone.
Janice, of course, but for all those friends and loved ones
who have shared my journey. You know who you are.

CHAPTER ONE

THERE was never much to do on a Sunday morning, except maybe to sit on a rocking chair, under the shade, and watch. Not that there was much to see either. The main street of 'Bethlehem' was empty, save for an old mule tied up outside Cecil Bowers' haberdashery store. The owner was nowhere to be seen. The 'Ruby Glow' saloon was closed, as were the adjacent shops. A horse whinnied from the yard of Hedgefield's livery and coral. Not much else though.

Reuben Cole leaned forward, chomping on his tobacco, and let loose a long brown stream of spittle into the street. Sitting back, he groaned, repositioned his hat and did his best to drift off to sleep. Ryan Stone, the young sheriff, newly appointed and as keen as anything, was out visiting the Gower sisters who had reported seeing a 'large black man' poking around in their apple orchard. Amelie, the younger of the two, brought in the news, nervous about leaving Claudette, her sister, out there on her own. Cole recalled the exchange. "Well, there is Joshua, of course, but Joshua is old now. Not sure what use he'd be in a fight."

"A fight?" Stone was busily writing the report down in a large ledger. That's the way things were done now, he had told Cole, everything had to be recorded.

"You said 'fight'. What sort of fight?" put in Cole.

"Oh, I don't know," said Amelie, all flustered. She wore a pretty sky-blue dress with white shawl and matching bonnet. A handsome woman, Cole estimated her age at around fifty and he didn't know of many much younger women who looked as fine as she. Except Maddie, of course. Amelie played with her folded parasol, rolling it in her palms, growing a little more nervous as she continued. "Gunfights and such."

Cole and Stone exchanged a look. "You think this intruder had a gun?" asked the young sheriff.

"Not sure," she said. "But he was black, so he must have."

Cole pulled a face. "Not sure I get your meaning there, ma'am."

"They *all* carry guns, don't they? Violent. Thieves and rapists the lot of them. Isn't that so?"

Suddenly Miss Amelie seemed a whole lot less attractive than before. Blowing out a long breath, Cole shot a glance towards Stone. "I'll be outside."

Later, with Amelie prancing off to the teahouse, Stone stepped out into the daylight, adjusting his gun belt. He checked his Colt Frontier. "She's worried," he said without lifting his head.

"Take the scatter-gun," Cole had suggested, already well ensconced in the rocking chair.

"No need for that Mr Cole, it's probably just some—"

"Humour an over-cautious old man," said Cole without shifting from his position. "Since that business of the break-in at the house, I'm kinda nervous about strangers rooting around." At this point, he tipped his hat back and settled a hard stare upon young Stone. "Take the scatter-gun."

Blowing out a sigh, but chuckling nonetheless, Stone did as asked. He went into the jailhouse and returned moments later with the gun, breaking it open to feed in the load. "You will look after the store whilst I'm gone?"

"Already am," said Cole, easing down the hat over his face, "already am."

That was almost three hours ago. A tiny tingling of something unsettling was becoming more noticeable at the nape of his neck. He didn't like the feeling and thought such things were way behind him. Farther than his neck anyway. Sniggering at his little private joke, he decided to give the young sheriff one more hour before he'd go take a look. Better safe than sorry.

From somewhere far off, the tiny clink of the church bell reminded himself that it was already noon and the padre had ended his service. Soon the faithful and the good would be traipsing back to their homes, and Myron would be opening the bar at the saloon. It was something to look forward to. Snuggling down, arms crossed, he tried again to sleep.

A loud, sharp retort caused him to spring upright, hat falling back. Instinctively, he reached for his gun, which was, as usual, adjusted for a cross-belly draw, the way it always had been since Cole's army days. Almost thirty years had slipped by since he stopped scouting for the United States Cavalry, but old habits do indeed die hard. If they didn't, it might be Cole who would be dying.

Blinking repeatedly, he climbed to his feet and stared in disbelief at the bizarre looking contraption trundling along the middle of the street. A curious, box-like construction, it appeared too flimsy to support the two adults squashed up inside. Open to the elements, they sat on a raised bench seat, covered in dark blue padding. A large, brightly chequered blanket covered their knees, and both wore hats and scarves. The man was the one steering the thing forward, if such a word could be used to describe the ongoing struggle he was making with the small wheel in front of him. Beside him, a slim, elegant looking woman, turned her smiling face towards Cole an action, which caused a tiny thrill to ripple through his abdomen. She possessed a sultry, breath-taking beauty, the kind men found irresistible.

The driver brought the beast to a halt, jerked on the handbrake, and reached to disengage the engine. Unfortunately, he was not fast enough to prevent another loud explosion and a rush of black smoke erupting from the machine's rear.

Clamping a gloved hand over her mouth, the woman stepped down, coughing hoarsely. A piece of black chiffon tied under her chin secured the bonnet. She wore a large grey overcoat, which fell to her ankles, encased as they were in laced patent black leather boots. Behind her, the man stepped up, rubbing his gloved hands together. He prised a set of goggles from his face and pushed them above the rim of his deerstalker cap. A two-piece gabardine coat completed his outfit, all designed to keep him warm and dry when he was perched on the machine's seat.

"Beautiful day," the man shouted. "We've been on the road for quite a while and would dearly love to stretch out legs, find a spot of something to eat. Drink. That sort of thing. Have you anything here?"

Cole couldn't quite catch the accent. He'd heard many in his time, but this one ... It sounded sing-song, like sailors from whaling ships he'd met years before, but a much stranger delivery of the vowels forcing him to strain to catch the meaning.

"If it's eating you're after ..." Cole paused for confirmation.

"Yes, indeed," said the woman, whose voice was clearly discernible. Almost melodic, Cole thought.

"Then you could try either the saloon, or Mrs Desmond, who opens her restaurant roundabout now to accommodate those returning from church."

"That sounds perfect," she said. Stepping forward,

she reached out her hand. "I am Mrs Cartwright, but you can call me Sarah." She gestured towards the man hovering at her side. "This is my husband Lewis."

The former scout took her hand and shook it. "I'm Cole."

"Pleased to meet you," she said, releasing her grip. "We've purchased the hotel and have made quite a trip from Nebraska, travelling in Lewis' beautiful horseless carriage here." She stepped aside to allow Cole an uninterrupted view. Lewis beamed, chest swollen with pride.

"Hotel? I didn't know it was for sale."

"Oh yes," said Lewis enthusiastically. He strode forward, proffering his hand this time. "Yes. The Elegance as it's called."

"Ah," said Cole, shaking his hand. "I know the one you mean, a little out of town, not so very far from the rail station?"

"That's the one. Perfect spot."

"It's a wonder nobody has snapped it up before now," put in Sarah Cartwright.

"Well, that could be because of the killing, but who knows."

"Killing?" The couple spoke as one and both looked shocked.

"Some time ago now," said Cole, "but I'm not too clear about the details, not being from here. I live quite a ways out of town myself, but in the opposite direction." To give some emphasis, he pointed towards the distant mountains.

"A killing?" Lewis turned away, shaking his head. "Nobody said anything about a killing ..." Swinging around again, he did his best to force a smile. "Still, it can't be haunted ... can it?"

"Who knows? Besides, wouldn't that be something of a selling point?"

"A selling poi—"

"Good Lord," interjected Sarah, "I think you could

have something there," and they all laughed. The mood broken, they bade their farewells and the couple walked off towards Mrs Desmond's restaurant. Cole returned to his rocking chair and, despite the welcome distraction of the newcomers, grew uneasy. Stone was now very much overdue, and he knew, if he didn't know before, that he would have to ride out there and check the situation. He'd promised himself not to get involved in such matters, but here he was once more, doing just that. He offered up a silent prayer that none of it would come to very much.

In that, he was to be proved wrong.

CHAPTER TWO

EVEN though the living nightmare of the proceeding weeks and months was to prove otherwise, initially it was just what they wanted. As soon as they stopped their carriage and took in the first, full view they both knew. It was instinctive. No words were needed. They simply turned to each other and smiled. In that smile was utter relief. Months of deliberation, arguing, doubting, had finally led them here. As far from the leafy avenues of Nebraska City as they could imagine. Nineteen Hundred and Five, but this area still felt very much like the Wild West. The untamed frontier. The town of Bethlehem, right on the border with Utah. An old mining town, but as close, both agreed, to perfect as they could wish as they craned their necks and took in the 'Elegance Hotel'.

With the money dear old, long forgotten Aunt Gwen left Lewis in her will, it was too good an opportunity to miss, especially with the promise it held for a good future. Fortunately, or so it appeared, Lewis agreed with his wife. Childless and reasonably happy, they had no one to consider but themselves. For the first time in their married life they could afford to take a gamble. They bought the 'Elegance' without a second

thought and with very little change left from the in-
heritance.

For over four years, or so they were told, the hotel
had stood empty. No one explained why, and certainly
not the agent who introduced them to the property.
"It's ideal," he said, rubbing his hands gleefully as the
couple studied the artist's drawing of the place. "The
railroad has only recently arrived and soon businesses
will take advantage. It's on a direct route to California,
and we all know about California, don't we."

The reality hit home as soon as the key fitted into
the front door and the door opened, the hinges
screaming their objection. A pungent smell of damp
and animal droppings immediately hit the back of their
throats. Sarah, gagging, held onto the closest wall, hand
across her mouth, eyes squeezed shut. "Oh my Lord,
Lewis. What *is* that smell?"

"Dead rats probably," he said. He marched forward,
taking in the surroundings, despite them being
shrouded in dust, cobwebs. Weak, sickly light trickled
in from the badly boarded up windows, but adequate
enough to pick out the details. "We've got some work
to do to get this place up and running."

Sarah moaned. "Haven't we just. It'll be worth it, in
the end. If we manage it."

He nodded. "If we don't, we could still make it
worthwhile." He kicked his boot through the thick
layer of white dust clinging to the floor. "It'll take a lot
of hard-work, darling. Elbow-grease and the like."

She did her best to smile, but barely managed little
more than a sneer.

During the subsequent weeks they would need to
spend ages scrubbing, repainting, fixing and replacing,
buying in new beds, furniture, fittings. None of it was
going to be quick, but they resigned themselves to
making a new life for themselves and both of them

were determined to do their very best to achieve their dream.

"You think that nice Mr Cole would help us?" Sarah asked as she trailed a forefinger through the grime of the reception counter.

"Possibly. He would certainly know of some labourers who could help."

"I'll ask him."

"Yes. But let's get our bearings first, yes? I'll check the upstairs rooms then we can begin to come up with some sort of plan."

Smiling, she watched him mounting the broad staircase to the first floor and wished she had invited Mr Cole to help them as soon as she'd met him.

CHAPTER THREE

THE heat pounded down upon him like a hammer of the gods, heavy and relentless. Soaked through with sweat, Cole did his best to maintain his speed but the longer the ride continued the more difficult this became. He decided not to veer off to his home. Maddie would be there, but she wouldn't expect him to turn up until the end of the day, knowing full well that Cole's helping hand to the young sheriff always took longer than anticipated. He found stomping around his father's big old house tedious and, since the break-in and all the horrors that ensued, he much preferred to be in town and while away his days, trying not to think of Maddie too much and the comforts of the wonderful home she had created for them both. But he was a troubled man, as Maddie herself often commented on. A man with a past he could not shake, of a life out on the open range. Army days, scouting days. So much to look back on. So, she encouraged him to go into town and sit, talk to those willing enough to engage him in conversation. Reminisce.

Nights, they were a different matter. The ghosts came then, as they always did, invading his mind. Images of his father and Sterling. Brown Owl. All those he'd lost. Maddie. She got sick soon after he returned following Sterling Roose's death, the news taking a lot out of her. He almost lost her too. Now, she was getting stronger every day. She made everything bearable, but only just.

Clearing his mind, he followed the trail to the Gower house, which was easy and didn't take much of Cole's considerable tracking skills. He prided himself he could still read the signs. Nowadays there was nobody else who had quite the degree of expertise as he. He often wondered if the Army ever came to ask him, would he offer his services. He was old now, early-sixties, and sitting all day in a saddle held little attraction for him. Even the gentle ride into town every morning took its toll on his limbs. Now, reining in his horse to consider the house, he rolled his shoulders and moved around on the hard saddle, trying to ease his discomfort. It didn't work.

The Gower place lay in a small depression. Attractive and well tendered, there were small fields set aside for potatoes, onions, cabbages and the like, a fruit orchard as well as surrounding borders of blooming flowers and shrubs. He marvelled at how the sisters had managed to create it all way out here in the scrub. He'd always thought of it as a lifeless place with no goodness in the ground, but there it was, like something out of one of those new-fangled special-interest magazines he sometimes saw in the mercantile store. Soon, within a generation he suspected, what with compulsory education, everyone would be able to read such things. An edition detailing gardens and gardening caught his eye. And here such a garden was, in all its beauty. A miracle to grow such wonders out here.

Despite the blaze of colour something disturbed him.

Nobody moved.

No signs of life.

He spotted the horses in the little coral, the assorted gardening equipment, the wheelbarrow. Reaching behind him he pulled out the telescope he'd been spurred on to purchase after that time with Marshal Whit back in the Seventies who'd used one to such good effect. A wonderful thing it was, even by modern standards. He pressed it against his eye and turned the focus ring to get a better idea.

The body lay face down, amongst the orchard trees, clearly dead. Cole never would have noticed it without the telescope.

Holding his breath, he scanned the rest of the area but saw nothing else. Except for the front door of the house slightly ajar.

That caused him deep concern and, groaning, he put the telescope away, exchanging it for his Winchester.

Easing his horse gently forward, about fifty or so paces from the silent cabin, Cole dismounted. Watchful, he stood behind his horse for a moment, checking for any movement or sound. There was neither. Scanning the surrounding expanse of open plain, he felt sufficiently secure to move forward, leading the horse to a clump of tangled trees. He threw the reins around the stoutest branch and continued on.

Ten paces or so from the building, he dropped to his knees, Winchester at his shoulder. He steadied his breathing.

There was nothing.

Keeping low, he edged across to the body in the field. It was an elderly black man, undoubtedly the servant Joshua. He'd been shot through the head, the exit wound having blown out most of his skull. The blood had dried hard and black, so this had happened some time ago. Buzzards had already started on the corpse. He saw the signs of human feet scampering away and there, not so far, the spent cartridge. Remaining where he was, Cole twisted himself to face the cabin. He spotted more tracks. Horses as well as human beings.

He pulled in a breath and crossed to the cabin. The porch was shaded by a large awning, supported by thick timber poles. A single step led up to the veranda. There was a wide, narrow, shuttered window to the left of the door and a stone chimney stack on the side. The roof was slate. This was a well-built, small yet elegant looking residence, not the usual sort of makeshift building settlers usually erected. With the threat of hostiles long gone, people felt a lot more confident now and were settling down to stay permanently. This would be a nice home to live in. Cole wondered if anybody lived in it now.

Tentatively, he put his weight on the step and hauled himself up to the veranda. A mournful sounding creak beneath him made him freeze, waiting. He had the Winchester at his side now, engaged, ready to fire. He moved towards the door.

He nudged open the door with the point of the Winchester's barrel. Again, the woodwork groaned, the hinges desperate for oil. The sound set his teeth on edge.

Inside, blackness. Not a breath of air stirred.

Waiting until his eyes adjusted to the gloom, he went inside.

Almost immediately he saw the man, slumped in the corner. Quickly checking the rest of the room, Cole crossed to him, put his fingers to the man's throat and felt the pulse. Acting fast now, he went to the window and opened up the shutters. Light flooded in and he turned to see the devastation.

Whatever had happened here had been swift and violent. Not a single piece of furniture or ornament re-mained upright. Whoever had done this had no regard for another person's property.

Again to the man. Cole saw it was Stone, the sheriff.

He was barely alive, a gunshot wound in his chest which must have missed his heart by inches. Outside, he'd noted the water trough, and he rushed to it, fetching water in a pail, returning to mop Stone's brow. Cole soaked up some water with his own neckerchief and squeezed drops from it onto Stone's lips. The man coughed and spluttered. Cole repeated the squeezing action until the man's eyes flickered open.

Seized by sudden fear, Stone panicked, gripping Cole's arm, crying out, "No, please!"

"It's all right, Ryan, it's me – Cole."

"Cole?" Stone's voice was nothing more than a strangulated croak, but his eyes were clearing, senses slowly returning. He shook his head repeatedly, groaning and wincing with pain. "They're here, Cole. They're here."

"No, it's all right. Whoever did this has gone."

Breathing in short, sharp gasps, Stone put his head back against the wall. "Oh God," he said. "I'm shot."

"Yes, you are, but it's gonna be all right. I'm gonna make you comfortable then go back to town and get the Doc."

"No," Stone said, his panic returning. He held onto Cole's arm, squeezing it tight. "No, you can't leave me. They'll come back, they'll—"

"Take it easy," said Cole, mopping Stone's glistening brow. "No one is coming back." He studied the up-turned room. "Where's the woman? Claudette?"

"They took her."

Cole snapped his head around to face Stone. "They *took* her?"

He nodded. Eyes closed again, face screwed up, his voice low and trembling as he spoke. "I rode up, not expecting to find anything. There were no horses, no signs anyone was here, but then I went up to the door, knocked on it and came in. She was in a chair, tied up. A man was slapping her, and she was crying. Another one turned to me as I went for my gun but a third one clubbed me on the back of the head." Unconsciously, he raised a hand to feel his skull. "I heard a gunshot from outside and although I was almost unconscious, I tried to pull my gun and that's when they shot me."

"Why did they take her?"

"Miss Claudette?" He shook his head. "They wanted the deed box, they said. I pretended to be out cold so I could hear 'em, every word. She wouldn't tell 'em so they tore the place apart. I heard 'em beating on her some more then she said it was in her lawyer's place and that's when I heard 'em taking her outside. She was kicking up one helluva fight, Cole, but nothing was gonna stop 'em." His eyes sprang open, feverishly locking in on Cole's own. "I couldn't do anything. I swear."

"Ryan, no one could have. You try and rest easy. Her lawyer's place, you say? Do you know where that is?" Stone shook his head. "Well, I could track 'em but it'll take some time. Further to that, they is killers so I'll need more men. Amelie is in town, she'll know where the lawyer is. I'll ride back, fetch the doc, then swear in some deputies for a posse. Meanwhile, I want you to sit here, try not to move. There's water," he tapped the pail, "and I'll find you a cup. I won't be long, you understand?"

Stone nodded, but then his face crumpled and tears sprang from his eyes. "Oh, Cole, I'm so sorry. I should have done more, been more cautious, but I never ..."

"You learn from this, Ryan. You hear me? You learn by your mistakes and you learn 'em fast. *Never* take things at face value, always be prepared and expectant. You're lucky, no one hardly gets a second chance out here." He stepped back, put a hand in the base of his spine and stretched out his muscles. "Darned if I don't feel like I been kicked by a mule. My old joints don't get any easier to move." He chuckled, despite the desperate situation. "I'll go. You hold on."

Stone gave a grudging nod as Cole searched around, found a tin cup, and pressed it into the young sheriff's hand. Without a further word, he went outside again.

Mounting up, Cole gave the surroundings one more scan. It would be simple enough to follow their tracks, but with the woman as hostage he could not take the risk of them spotting him before he got too close. If he was forced to go up against them, he'd need men, good men.

He pulled a face and kicked his horse into a gallop.

It was Nineteen-Hundred and Five. He doubted there were any 'good men' left.

CHAPTER FOUR

NOT everyone in the town was enthusiastic over the re-opening of the Elegance Hotel. Following the church service, words were exchanged between parishioners as they strolled out into the sunshine. The Preacher, Mr Peters, who called himself 'Reverend' – a man not unused to a good drink himself – listened to the comments with feigned interest.

"I'm not sure if it's a good thing," Mrs Collins was saying on her way out. "No doubt they're very nice people, but the town doesn't need that sort of..." She struggled for a moment to find the appropriate word that would convey the depth of her feeling. Not finding one she settled for, "that sort of *thing*."

Her point, if not her use of language, was shared by Mrs Daniels, a stout woman, all full-length overcoat and heavy eyebrows, whose own husband had died two years earlier due to, she maintained, the 'demon drink.' "We don't want drunkards here. Keep them up-country, that's my view."

"They're hardly that, Mrs Daniels," began the Reverend, marvelling at the woman's ability not to perspire, or even look remotely heated in such a coat on such a day. He almost instantly regretted his interjection, however, as the formidable Mrs Daniels fired him a vicious glare. She disliked this preacher, disliked his youthfulness, his 'new' way, his desire to attract more people into the church by offering guitars, choruses, clapping. She bristled with indignation. "I know what I'm talking about, Mr Peters," she said and, wishing him a good morning, she departed. Mrs Collins watched her go. "Nothing good will come of this, Reverend."

"It is only a hotel, Mrs Collins. You never know, it might do the town some good."

"I don't see how. Drink and debauchery never did anybody any good."

"Mrs Collins that is a misplaced and rash judgement if I may say so. I am sure the owners will have nothing to do with such excesses." She didn't look convinced, but he plunged on regardless. "With the ever-expanding railroad system, the town needs a place for businessmen and the like to stay on their way farther west, or even south. It will bring well-needed business to the town."

Pursing her lips, she said, "Where are they from anyway?"

"Not from here, I know that much. East I should imagine, or somewhere up north."

"M'mm, that doesn't tell me a lot. Do they know the history of the place?"

"Now *that* I couldn't say."

"Then it might be a good idea if somebody told them, don't you think?"

The Reverend blinked. "You mean *I* should?"

"Mr Peters, it really is your duty, would you not agree?"

The Reverend wouldn't, but he remained silent.

Mrs Collins nodded to him. Her views concerning him were not as strong as Mrs Daniels', but nevertheless she had her suspicions. She reluctantly supported the Reverend's plans for the re-structuring of services to attract the young to the congregation. No, it was the *man*. She knew about his drinking, of course, but she also knew that it was never to excess. What she didn't like was his idea of creating a boxing club. Wayward young men frequented the old barn just outside the town where they would *train*. She had no idea what that term meant but she felt there was something not quite right about a man of God who kept his body in such good shape, whose swollen chest and shoulders strained against the seams of his vestments and whose hands so obviously bore the marks of manual labour. Here was a man who had a past, a past that was so annoyingly shrouded in mystery. "I shall see you on Tuesday evening for Bible class, Mr Peters. You could tell me their reaction to the news then. Good day."

The Reverend Peters rarely swore, not because of any pious feelings he had on the subject but simply because he was usually unruffled by most of life's little setbacks so had little need to vent his anger with expletives. This, however, was no such moment. He hissed a curse through his teeth before dipping back inside his church. He stood for a moment in the still, stark silence and closed his eyes, drinking in the quiet, allowing the atmosphere to gently waft over him, calm and cool him. The greatest drawback of living in such a small, introvert place was the gossip. It was rampant. And here he was, stuck in the middle, hating it all and yet knowing that now it was up to him to let the Cartwrights know what it was they were living amongst. Forgotten dreams – or, more aptly, nightmares. Perhaps not even forgotten, at least not by the Mrs Collins of this world. He opened his eyes. Why don't people just let go? Why do they cling on to the past, especially the bad parts? Why couldn't the Cartwrights be left in blissful ignorance and why couldn't he find the courage to tell Mrs Collins to go and tell them the story herself? It was all so unnecessary. But what was he to do? He said he would tell them. There was no going back.

He moved down the aisle, sweeping his eyes across

the tiny altar. People said it was pre-Revolution. He couldn't imagine anyone living out here back then. He let out a sigh, turned around and leaned back against the cold stone. The dark, yet comforting expanse stretched out before him, rows of pews reeking of history, thousands of ghostly backsides having left their impressions on those polished wooden seats. It was a sobering thought the knowledge that so many had come to this place to find solace, release, hope...all of them looking to preachers not unlike himself for help, guidance, faith. It was a heady responsibility he bore and people, past and present, expected so much from those like him. For the sake of his predecessors he would have to do it. He smiled, finding reassurance in their silent support. He thrived on responsibility. It was what made his calling – for that was how he viewed his work in the Church. So worthwhile, so challenging. God would be his rock and life, as always, and giving the Cartwrights an insight into their new purchase would not prove to be as bad as he thought.

He hoped, because he too had nightmares. Sometimes, the past came to visit, to seize him in its horrible embrace. Faith often came to his aide but recently the memories reared up too strong and so relentless.

He took a deep breath and decided he would go and see the Cartwrights that very afternoon. If he could manage to get this evening's sermon down on paper before then, perhaps he could take a drink or two with the newcomers.

Peters allowed himself a smile. No, life wasn't really all that bad at all.

CHAPTER FIVE

"That's the lot," called Sarah Cartwright as she came round from behind the bar, drying her hands on a towel. She'd decided to work on the reception area before anything else as it would be the first thing potential customers would see and she was anxious to get things moving. A selling point, you could say. An advert. Upstairs, Lewis busied himself in the second of the rooms. Top of the list, he'd cleaned a single, which had proved reasonably easy, but the double was a struggle to prepare. A gaping hole in the roof allowed dust and debris to pile up in the corners, putting a thick film of dirt over everything. As he clumped down the stairs of the two storey hotel, he forced a smile when he saw Sarah with her hair tied back, wearing green overalls, which disguised her fine figure, sleeves rolled up past her elbows. Her determination to make the hotel a success was an inspiration.

Ten years her husband's junior, she was a tall, slim, elegant woman. When not pulled back like now, a cascade of full, brown locks tumbled down around her shoulders, framing her elfin face, producing quite devastating effects on any man that laid eyes on her. Lewis had noted how that old man, Cole, had stopped, mesmerised by her. Lewis had to admit he didn't like it and wondered, not for the first time, if this was the type of business they should be embarking upon. A business which demanded polite and efficient responses from both the owners. He wasn't too sure about that. Sarah always found being friendly so very easy, lapping up those puppy-dog eyes and the drooling mouths, but Lewis, not the most out-going of people, despised it. Not at all gregarious, he preferred to be out of the public eye, locked away in his office, concentrating on the accounts. He found comfort in the knowledge that if they discovered what it was that had brought them here, he could employ an army to keep the place up and running.

Sarah mentioned that once they opened and business developed, they would need to employ additional staff. Already a cook had appeared, the one who had answered their initial newspaper advertisement. Nearly sixty, Blanche Chambers was on trial, preparing them dinner in the compact kitchen. She too had worked tirelessly to ensure the place was ready, at one point emerging, bathed in sweat, a dishevelled mess but beaming nevertheless. "I don't believe that stove has been used for years."

Smiling, Sarah put down her cleaning cloth, held out her hand to Lewis and pulled him to her. "Why don't we all have a little break?"

He kissed her, winked at Blanche, and agreed.

They sat around a small table. Lewis supplied glasses of cold beer and, for a moment at least, a sense of calm settled over them.

"It's a beautiful place," said Blanche, allowing her eyes to roam through the foyer, past the reception desk, the bar, and up the narrow staircase. "How many rooms is it?"

"Twelve," said Lewis.

"Six singles and six doubles," added Sarah. "It's enough."

"If things go well," continued Lewis, "we could build an extension. But we'll see."

"It all depends on what happens after the railroad opens up here. We got in touch with them and they say it'll be no longer than six-moths."

"Well," said Blanche, finishing her beer. "The station is completed. Very fine it looks."

Lewis studied her lined face. He pondered with the thought that a much younger, more attractive barmaid might take some of the attention away from his wife. But he doubted that. Sarah was still the most sensual woman he had ever seen and the fact that most other men agreed with him caused him no end of stress. How much longer would it be, he again mused, before some younger, fitter, and more able man moved in and gave her what she so obviously needed and what he found so increasingly difficult to deliver?

His thoughts were dispelled when Blanche declared that she must "Get on!" and Lewis finished his beer, watched her leave with the empty plates and sat back, sighing. "How long is it all going to take?"

"A couple of weeks," said Sarah. "This reception area needs repainting, furniture replacing, carpets cleaned. It's going to be a full-time job, Lewis."

A thought struck him, and he stood up. "I'm taking a look down below," he said. "For all we know it'll be in a worse state than anywhere."

"Be careful. Take a lamp with you."

Doing as she suggested, Lewis descended into the dark cellar. He had been down there before, during their first inspection of the property in fact, but he still wasn't absolutely certain of his way round. Holding the oil-lamp aloft, he could make out shapes of stacked-up chairs, boxes, rolled up carpets, lots and lots of rotting ledgers and barrels of indeterminate age, which no doubt held beer once. And the smell, thick, heavy. It settled in the back of his throat, causing him to cough intermittently. But there was something else which gripped him. A feeling of unease he couldn't shift. The place had an atmosphere that made it seem strangely out of tune with the rest of the house. He looked about him and through the half-gloom he could just make out a set of dust-encrusted racks on which lay half a dozen or more bottles of some long-forgotten wine. The wood looked rotten, as did everything else. Nothing had been looked at since the place was shut up. He inched forward. Those barrels, precariously stacked, leaned at an impossible angle against the far wall. He rapped one with his knuckles. They were not empty, but what they held only the Lord knew. Lewis sighed heavily. They would all have to be cleared out. During the week, once the rooms were done, he would have to spend some time down here, cleaning, putting in gas lights, trying to make it presentable. His thoughts drifted away, picturing what it must have been like years ago. Who visited then, he wondered, before the War, before it happened. Did it happen down here, amongst the detritus and the dust? Perhaps in the dark, all sound lost in the depths of this mournful place. The sound of the screams. There must have been screams, he assumed...

"Lewis, where have you got to?"

Sarah's voice broke through his thoughtful meandering. He was doing that more and more frequently, he said to himself in a form of admonishment. Forever daydreaming, he must have been down here in the dark for longer than he thought. He really must concentrate on what he's doing.

"Lewis, what are you doing down there? We have the rooms to finish."

"Yes. Just coming."

As he returned to the muggy air of the reception, he noticed that her face had that barely controlled look about it, the look that spelled trouble no matter what the explanation for his prolonged absence might be.

"Sorry," he offered limply, and she retorted with her usual, "You will be." He steeled himself to concentrate on the business in hand and stomped upstairs to face the rooms once again. The images of the cellar, however, kept coming back into his head. What was wrong with it? He'd never felt this way about any other place in his entire life. He stood for a while, absently polishing a wall mirror, wondering if there was any way he could find out more, perhaps discover something that would give him the answer to his dread feelings. Whatever it was couldn't linger there. What had happened, the sketchy details he knew about, was over. Gone forever. Ghosts didn't exist. It was only a cellar, he convinced himself – what could possibly be wrong with a cellar? He turned and pulled off the bed sheets, gave an involuntary shiver, considered asking Sarah's opinion, quickly thought better of that and threw himself into his work.

CHAPTER SIX

BEFORE the horse came to a halt, Cole was swinging himself from the saddle. The impact jolted his old bones and he winced, cursing himself for being so dismissive of his aches and pains. There was nothing he could do about the fact that he was getting older. He couldn't remember the last time he'd spent a prolonged time in the saddle, but he needed to remember because the physical effort brought agony to his muscles and limbs. Right now, he needed to focus so, gritting his teeth, he stretched out his back, put the pain out of his mind and went through the door of Doc Wycliffe's surgery.

"What can I do for you, Reuben?" came the shrill voice of Mrs Nelson, the receptionist, who had taken up her usual defensive position behind her desk. A small shrew of a woman, she was nevertheless formidable and only allowed those with an appointment or the most urgent of cases to pass through to the inner sanctum. It was all the thing in New York City, she'd announced, and what was good out east was just as good here.

"We'll be making appointments by telephone soon," said Mrs Tomes one sun-baked morning.

Twisting her lips into what she considered a smile,

Mrs Nelson waggled her finger, "Why Geraldine that is *exactly* what Doctor Wycliffe is looking into."

But this was now, and at this moment Cole appeared more agitated than usual.

"You look somewhat flustered, Reuben. Can I be of assistance?"

Cole told her as best he could and, without any discussion, she went directly into Wycliffe's consulting room and within seconds he was out front, glaring at the former Army scout. "The sheriff, you say?"

"He's been shot. It looks bad and I didn't want to bring him as it's in the chest and—"

"Yes, yes, quite so, Reuben. I'm well aware of your knowledge of such things. Where is he?"

"I left him at the Gower's place."

"Amelie?" said Mrs Nelson, looking astounded. "Why, I have only just seen her—"

"I know the place," said Wycliffe, dismissing his receptionist's comment with a wave of the hand. "I'll get my bag and ride on out there. Mrs Nelson, prepare everything for further surgery on my return."

Knowing he could do no more, Cole made his excuses and left. He crossed to the Sheriff's office and eased open the door. He scrambled around, trying to find the appropriate forms. Everything was forms these days. At the back of a desk drawer, he found what he was looking for. Grabbing a pencil stub, he made his way to the saloon.

It being late afternoon the place was fairly full. Something of a private individual who found making a public address difficult, Cole preferred to approach individuals personally, briefly explaining the situation, inviting each to sign up as temporary deputies.

He gained one volunteer.

Keeping his temper, Cole led the man outside. "Best if we talk out here," he said.

"That's fine by me."

"What's your name?"

"Sebastian Monroe. My friends call me Seb, most others just plain Monroe."

"Well, until we're better acquainted ... have you ever used firearms, Monroe?"

"I was in the Army," Monroe said, pulling out a cheroot. He rammed it into the corner of his mouth and lit it. "Fought at Sugar Point. Not something I remember with much fondness. After that, I got myself a job working for the railroad. Shot two men trying to hold up the train just east of here. That'd be ... Nineteen Oh-two."

"Why you give it up?"

Monroe shrugged. "I told 'em I was no assassin and if they wanted to employ me as such they should pay me at least ten times more."

"So, they asked you to leave."

"No severance, nothing." He blew out a stream of smoke. "Since then I been doing odd-jobs here and there. I sometimes serve whisky and beer behind the bar. Been looking at that new hotel. Maybe they might need someone."

"Could be. This job for me – well, for the Sheriff. It's voluntary. No pay."

"But you'd give me a reference for those hotel people?"

"The least I can do."

"So, when do we leave?"

CHAPTER SEVEN

THE day dawned as bright and as clear as any she could remember. She stood on the porch, breathing in the clean air, her eyes wandering over the rambling plains beyond the town limits. This was a staggeringly beautiful place and, if she did have doubts, they were now dispelled. This had been a good move. A decision well made.

She heard the footfall behind her and turned to see Lewis, stretching and yawning as he joined her.

"Isn't it just the most perfect place?" she asked him, slipping her arms around his waist, drawing him close.

"It is," he said, pressing his face into her hair. He kissed her.

"We're going to be happy here."

"Yes," he said. "But it's going to mean a lot of hard work. I've written a letter to the railroad company, asking them about advertising rates. In England they have posters advertising places to visit and where to stay plastered over every station. I'm wondering if our railroad might do the same."

"We'll put more ads in the newspapers back in Kansas. Chicago too. When the line finally opens, we could be inundated."

"We could find an artist to paint pictures, to really

sell the place in the adverts I'm proposing." Lewis smiled, allowing his mind to conjure up mountains of dollar bills.

"You really have it all planned out, don't you, my love."

"Well," he chuckled, "let's wait and see."

She drew in a deep breath. "I'm going out this afternoon, if you want anything to eat, I've left you some stew on the hot-plate."

"Thanks. Where're you going?"

She swung away and went back inside, her voice was receding as she climbed the stairs to the bathroom, freshly prepared by her own hand the night before. "Miss Gower said she would give me a guided tour of the town, show me the sights so to speak."

"Very good of her, whoever she is," he was shouting now. "When will you be back?"

"No idea." There was a pause. "Don't worry, I'll get back to work as soon as I return."

"I didn't doubt it..."

He sat down on the porch rocking chair. He heard her moving about upstairs, then the steady thump of her descent.

She appeared all of a sudden, flowing skirt, cream blouse, hair pulled back off her face and tied up with a bow. She looked stunning. "Well?"

He shook his head, his throat sounding constricted when he said, "You look lovely."

She snapped her handbag shut, lay her finger to her lips and then touched his nose as she drifted past him. "Have a nice day, dear." She smiled at him as she went down the steps to the street, almost immediately colliding with the Reverend Peters as he appeared seemingly from nowhere.

"Oh my word!" she hissed, pulling back her feet from under his.

"I'm terribly sorry," he said in a whirl wind of arms,

awkward grins, and embarrassed little laughs. "Is your husband...?"

"I'm here," said Lewis quickly coming off the rocking chair, anxiously checking that Sarah was still in one piece after colliding with the powerfully built preacher. Ignoring them both, Sarah strutted towards the main street, tossing her head, unhappy. "I'm afraid," Lewis continued, eyeing her with concern, "we're not yet open..." He glanced at the Reverend's dog-collar and added, "Padre."

"Oh, I realise that. No, no, I'm here in a, how shall I call it, an advisory capacity?"

Lewis noted the tone of uncertainty, and the preacher's air of awkwardness which, he felt sure, wasn't due to his collision with Sarah. "Advisory capacity? I'm not altogether sure if I understand you, Padre."

"Well, that could be the wrong word... Perhaps it's not advisory at all. I really only popped in for a sort of little get-to-know each other chat, sort of thing."

Lewis looked at the Reverend as if for the first time. "Your accent? English?"

"Borders. Scottish borders, I mean. Berwick. You know it?"

Lewis shook his head. "I'm afraid we're not particularly religious, either of us."

"No, no," the Reverend nodded his large head, but the smile never left his face. "I'm not really here for that. Just a chat. About...about the history of the hotel really."

"Oh." Lewis's interest began to stir. "Perhaps you'd better come in."

The Reverend Peters dipped his head and stepped into the murky interior. The ceiling was low, especially for such a big man. The Reverend smiled uneasily as Lewis brushed past him. "I haven't been here for such a long time," Peters said with a faint note of sadness, "I'd almost forgotten what it looks like."

Lewis motioned him into the lounge, almost complete now with an abundance of comfortable looking seating, card tables by the windows, empty fireplace due to the heat. An inviting ambience, or so Lewis liked to think. "You used to come quite often then, Padre?"

"I'm afraid so, yes." He gave a little nervous laugh. "The saloon is not really a place I would ever consider frequenting. I'm not a great drinker, but I do like the occasional snifter...I'm sure you know what I mean."

Lewis thought he did. He pulled up a chair and they both sat. He had an innate distrust of clergy, of whatever denomination. He always felt he was being scanned, as if by some device that could read his very soul. They all had that air of grace, of invulnerability that Lewis found haughty, almost arrogant.

He took in a deep breath and looked at the man who settled himself somewhat awkwardly into the big armchair opposite him. Smiling, prepared to give the Reverend the benefit of the many doubts he had, Lewis said, "So, you have some history to tell me, about the hotel?" He smiled and waited. The Reverend's unease became palpable and Lewis suddenly began to suspect that what he was about to hear would be distasteful.

"Yes, yes I have." The Reverend took in a large breath as if preparing himself for the delivery of something astonishing. "It's about the murder actually."

CHAPTER EIGHT

ITCHING their horses outside the Gower's place, Cole and Monroe waited patiently for Amelie to arrive in the buggy, a buggy driven by another woman, one whom Cole recognised as Sarah Cartwright, the new owner of the Elegance Hotel. She took all of his attention as she stepped down, extended her hand to Amelie and helped the older lady to join her.

Cole doffed his hat. "Good morning to you both, ladies."

Amelie appeared deeply troubled, wringing her hands, all pretence of social etiquette absent. "Mr Cole, I do not understand any of this. When you announced to me earlier that there was trouble, I had no idea you meant here, in my home!"

"I apologize to you, Miss Amelie, but time was pressing. Now that we are here, I will—"

"Perhaps if you just tell us what has happened?" It was Sarah, her voice liquid velvet. Cole noted how her gaze was fixed upon Monroe, who, he also noted, wore a wide smile, as if transfixed. "I don't think I've had the pleasure," she said, extending her hand.

Monroe took it and, to the surprise of Cole and

everyone else, pressed the hand to his lips and kissed it. "The pleasure is all mine."

Clearing his throat, Cole stepped aside and beckoned for Amelie to enter. "Sheriff Stone is inside. He'll let you know the details, but please try and be—" He did not make the end of his sentence as, with a toss of her head, Amelie strode into the cabin with Sarah Cartwright close behind, leaving the two men to watch them.

Monroe pursed his lips and emitted a silent whistle. "Dear Lord, she is the most beautiful woman I think I've ever seen!"

Cole gave him a sideways glance. "You'd do best to keep your admiration to yourself. She's a married woman."

"Ah Reuben," said the much bigger man, clamping his hand on the ex-scout's shoulder, "I'm young and headstrong. I can't help myself." He chuckled. "And neither can she, I shouldn't wonder."

Cole considered what a dreadful error of judgement he'd made in enlisting this grossly conceited man's help. He wanted to say something but knew this was not the time nor the place, so he let it go and went into the cabin.

Inside, the air was thick and stuffy. Despite one of the tiny windows being wedged open, the gloom shrouded everything, lending it a depressed, unfriendly and uninviting atmosphere. In the back room the women had gathered. Amelie was crying quietly into a handkerchief, Sarah Cartwright doing her best to comfort her. In the bed, ghastly pale, Sheriff Ryan Stone and standing before them, Doc Wycliffe.

"He's comfortable now," Wycliffe was saying, as he came out of the room, rolling his sleeves down over his thick forearms. "I have to say it was touch-and-go for a moment, but he's young and he's strong. He'll make it."

"Thanks, Doc."

"It's my job, Cole. Yours is to hunt down the varmints that did this."

"I will."

Grunting, Wycliffe studied Monroe from head to toe. "This your deputy?"

"The only one I could muster."

"Good luck with that then," he said and slinked off.

"What in the hell did he mean by that?" demanded Monroe, looking as if he was about to follow the good doctor and accost him.

"Perhaps you could tell me."

A deep frown appeared on Monroe's face. "Listen, I'm the only one who stepped up when you came asking. You'd do well to remember that, old man."

"Ah. Really?"

"You're damned right!"

The big man's hand hovered close to the Police Special at his waist, the type of firearm Sterling Roose had taken to wearing in the later stages of his life, before all of that came to an abrupt and dreadful end. Pegged out to dry in the baking sun like some buffalo skin. Cole drew in a breath, swallowing down the memory of his old friend. "Tell you what, Monroe, we ride, you follow. And in the meantime, keep your mouth shut."

"You think a lot of yourself, don't you, old man? People say you used to hunt Indians."

"Do they?"

"Yeah, they do. They say you killed a lot of men, but that was ages ago, they say. Now, all you do is rock in your chair and pass the time of day chewing backy. You is passed it now."

Cole's eyes narrowed and all of a sudden, he no longer felt old at all. "Let's just see, shall we."

"Yeah. We shall. And when we find these killers, it'll be me who brings it to an end, you can trust me on that."

"Yeah, because you were at that battle, weren't you."

"Sugar Point. That's right."

Cole went to turn away, but pulled up when Monroe said, "How many battles you been in, eh?"

Cole turned, and let out a long sigh. "Enough."

The big man didn't look as if he believed the ex-scout's words, but Cole was no longer in the mood to exchange niceties. He went into the back room to check on Stone.

"Why hello there, stranger," said Stone. Propped up with a mass of pillows, Sarah sat beside him while Amelie fussed around, pulling out drawers and opening wardrobe doors.

Cole grinned and raised his hand. "Ryan, can you tell me any more about the men who came here?"

"Not much more than I told you before. There were three of them. Two white guys and one enormous Negro. They were looking for something and didn't care who they hurt to find it."

"Including Claudette," said Amelie. She came away from the wardrobe she'd been looking through. "Why did they take her?"

"Kidnapped her," emphasised Stone. "No doubt to hold her to ransom, for whatever it is they are seeking."

"But what can it be," said Amelie, her voice high-pitched, close to breaking. She slumped down on the bed. "We're not wealthy. Everything we had we put into this place. And why gun down Joshua the way they did? It is all so senseless."

"Whatever it is they're looking for," said Cole, "it is worth killing for. These are desperate men, capable of anything."

"But this isn't the Wild West," said Sarah. She looked concerned, perspiration across her top lip. This was not what she wanted to find when she decided to open up the hotel. From her expression that much was clear.

"It still ain't tamed," said Cole, "and I doubt it'll be for a long, long time."

Amelie said, "What if they murder Claudette?"

Cole did his best to sound reassuring, but he was no actor and his words failed to have any impression upon the younger sister. "I doubt it, Miss Gower. What would be the point in that?"

"What is the point in *any* of this?"

To that Cole had no answer. These were two spinsters, living alone in this well-appointed home, comfortable but not wealthy. Desperate men, looking to make some quick money, don't break in, kill and kidnap unless there is something worthwhile to be had.

"Miss Gower," said Stone from the bed, voice strained but under control. "Are you certain there were no valuables in the house — jewellery, cash, anything at all."

"Nothing, Sheriff. We are simple folk trying to live out our lives in peace and quiet."

"Besides," put in Sarah, "they surely would know if there was something here, wouldn't they?"

"You're right, Mrs Cartwright. I can't believe this was a random raid," said Stone. "Mr Cole, I will be well enough to ride soon. If you would prefer to wait a little while, I will join you in bringing these men to justice."

"The longer we wait the farther away they get."

"Yes," Stone said, resigned to the reality of the situation. "But you have only one man. I'm not doubting your desire, nor your experience, but—"

"You're no longer young," put in Amelie. She held up her hand as Cole went to speak. "I have heard all about you, Mr Cole. How you tracked down villains and savages and the like, how you mercilessly served justice, but the last time you went up against such men was—"

"Less than a year ago," said Cole quickly, anxious not to listen to any more of this diatribe. "I went to the aid of my old friend, Sterling Roose."

"Yes ..." Amelie Gower's voice trailed away. "Mr Roose was a good sheriff I have no doubt, but the fact that both of you were very much out of your depth just goes to show how age weakens us all, Mr Cole, in so many ways."

"Out of my depth." Cole blew out a long sigh. "Miss Gower, I shot the whole damn lot of 'em. Dead. Now, if you'll excuse me, I have a job to do."

He shot Stone a look, knowing the young sheriff knew the truth of what had happened, and left, leaving Amelie Gower shocked, speechless in fact, and Sarah moved to put her arm around her and give some sense of comfort.

CHAPTER NINE

SARAH Cartwright made Amelie and Stone tea before stepping outside to gaze across the empty land over which Cole and his companion had travelled across. Her mind drifted to other things. Not for the first time, she dwelled on the moment when she had accidentally collided with the preacher. For only the fleeting of instances they pressed together, but in that brief blink of time she had felt the force of his form, sensed the strength of his arms, explored the hard flatness of his stomach. The sensation had thrilled her. It had been two years since she had buried thoughts of the episode that had almost cost her her marriage. She made promises both to herself and Lewis that it would never happen again. However, sweet memories often invaded her sleeping moments, and she knew it was folly to deny simple facts. Lewis was a good, hardworking man, but attentive he was not. He could not tame her wayward spirit.

But could a preacher?

She put such thoughts out of her mind. This was a new place, a chance to start again. She was determined to do all she could to make the hotel a success. Her marriage too. Lewis was under stress. That was all it was. Things would change, of course they would. All it would take was time.

A voice cut into her thoughts causing her to jump. "Sarah, have they gone?"

Amelie's usually good-humoured face appeared lined with worry and strain. "Yes," said Sarah. "I hope they return with good news."

"I pray for that. Claudette is not as strong as she was. I'm worried."

She pulled up a chair and sat beside Sarah on the porch.

"This was a good place," she said quietly. "We had so many hopes and dreams. Joshua was a godsend, working such long hours, without complaint. It's terrible what those monsters did, to butcher him like ... like some poor, wretched animal."

"He must have tried to stop them."

"Yes, and they cut him down and left him to bleach in the Sun." Convulsed with a fresh bout of despair, she pressed a sodden silk handkerchief into her eyes. "Why did this have to happen?"

"I don't know. It seems this town isn't tamed at all. It's still part of the Wild West, isn't it?"

"The Wild West? The stuff of legends, so they'd have you believe. Newspapers and dime novels making it out to be so terribly romantic. Bank robbers, gun-fighters, lawmen. It's all too easy to let yourself believe none of it actually happened. But it did happen – and it's still happening."

"You're right. We succumbed to the lure of a good life, of wide-open spaces, of fresh air and endless oppor-tunity. We were so full of hope – my husband and I. We planned to make a real go of the hotel. We were assured Colorado was tamed, but from what Mr Cole intimated at, it is far from the rural idyll the real estate people sold us back in Kansas City."

"They're all vultures those types, only out to get as much money from you as they can."

"We thought we got it at a good price. The hotel I mean. It's very fine. Perhaps once it is ready we can put aside fears and concerns and make it into something special."

"Yes, once the railroad is opened. That's the reason you bought it, so I've heard? The promise of a steady stream of customers?"

"Word gets around fast, doesn't it?"

"A new face in this little place sticks out a mile, especially when it's one as beautiful as yours, Sarah. People are naturally curious, and what with your horseless carriage trundling down the main street, news was bound to travel very quickly."

It was an uneasy feeling, this knowledge that everybody knew you but you knew nobody. Sarah did her best to conceal her unease. What else were they saying, she wondered.

"You'll make a success of it all, I know you will," Amelie remarked

"It'll require plenty of hard work before it'll be ready for opening. But we'll do it. Lewis is very determined."

"Is he?"

"Oh, yes. He wants the elegance to be a success. So do I," Sarah said.

"And what happened, none of that concerns you at all."

"We don't know any of the details. I'm not at all sure if anything actually did happen."

"Oh, it most certainly did, Sarah."

"I'm intrigued."

"Both Claudette and I have talked about how we believed the Territory to be a peaceful place now. But after the dreadful incident with my sister and Joshua, I'm not so sure. What happened here, in the hotel, was not, as most of us hoped, the last stain on our community." Wringing her hands, she turned away, voice tremulous. "Killings, robberies, all of that. Things buried deep. But now ... now, those blights, they have returned." She looked again at Sarah. "This is not the tranquil place it appears to be. I don't suppose it ever was."

"A stain, you said. What sort of stain?"

"It's not an easy tale to tell. I hope I'm doing the right thing if I tell you." Amelie looked up quickly. "Not that I don't trust you, it's not that, it's...it's...Well, it might affect the way you look at things, how you conduct your new life." She pulled in a deep, troubled breath, suddenly making up her mind. She began tentatively, introducing the main characters, the time, the situation – as far as she was aware that is – and then recounted the full horror of what had happened.

CHAPTER TEN

COLE returned to his horse and stood there for a moment, contemplating the saddle. He felt tired and worried.

"What's wrong?"

Cole turned to Monroe, sitting big and proud on the back of his horse. He looked bored but not tired. Alert, as if he expected something. Cole didn't know what, but his unease grew with each passing minute he shared in this man's company. "Tracks," he said quietly and heaved himself into his saddle.

"What, you mean signs?"

"That's right."

"So, we're on the right path?"

"They ain't making any secret of where they're heading. But one of them is on foot."

"Could be the woman."

"That's my thinking too. She's old, and I'm not sure how much she can take out in this heat." To give his words more weight, he took off his hat and wiped his forehead with his neckerchief. "How are you holding up?"

"Oh, you've no need to worry about me, Mr Cole. I'm well used to living it rough."

"I don't doubt it."

He kicked his horse's flanks and moved on.

The air hummed with the intensity of the sun. Keeping his eyes on the ground, Cole noted how the tracks changed. Those he pursued were slowing to a walk. Soon they would be within sight, then he would need to decide what to do. Three of them, Stone said, but the woman was the problem. Once any shooting started, she would be the first to die. He'd need to wait until nightfall, creep up on them in a surprise attack. He hoped his old bones would respond positively. The thought of crawling over the hard, baked earth was not something he relished.

He took his horse up a sharp incline, away from the fresh, clear tracks. In his bedroll was his telescope, the one which had served him so well over the years. If he could find an advantageous position, he may well be able to figure out how far away they were and how best to overcome them.

As it was, as he reached the top, he had no need for the 'scope.

They were camped in a small dip, sat around an open fire, something roasting on a makeshift spit.

Three men.

To their right, a bundle. A white bundle, big enough to be a person.

Reaching for his telescope, he focused in and sucked in a sharp breath.

It was a woman. Clearly Claudette. She appeared unconscious, lying there in the open, not moving.

Was she dead?

Cursing, Cole snapped shut the telescope and twisted around to face the sound of Monroe's approaching steps. "It seems like—" he began, but got no further.

The stock of the Winchester smashed hard into his

face, and he fell back with a loud grunt, senses swirling, flashes of blinding pain overcoming his vision.

Something moved. He knew not what. Strong hands lifted him, Monroe's voice from a hundred miles away saying, "You're too old for this sort of thing now, Cole." And a fist erupting into his guts, jack-knifing him forward. A hand under his chin. Lifting his face. Through bleary, tear-ridden eyes, he managed to make out Monroe. Grinning. Big and burly. Why did he ever recruit him? He should have known, he should have—

The shape of a large fist filled his world. Then the impact. Massive. Total. Smashing bone, clattering his brain around in his skull, pitching him into a whirlwind of blackness, dragging him forever downwards.

He came to hours, perhaps, for all he knew, days later.

On his back, blinking at the sun. A huge, white orb, searing through his face, a face pulsing with pain.

Rolling over onto his side, he let out a prolonged groan and vomited onto the earth. Coughing, he lay that way for some time, struggling to find the strength to sit up. Desperate for water. Desperate for understanding of what had happened. Desperate for sleep.

He succumbed.

The next time he woke, it was almost night, the sun low on the horizon. Late evening. An hour of weak daylight left at best. A buzzard, a huge thing, yellow, virulent eyes studying him, stood only inches away. He shouted, made a wild swipe with his hand, and it screeched, flew backwards a couple of paces, then settled again. To wait. It knew something. Something that perhaps Cole hadn't yet guessed.

He forced himself to sit up. A great sledgehammer of pain exploded through his jaw. Monroe must have hit him with his Winchester, the one he'd left with his horse as he reached the top of the hill and crawled to take a look over the edge. To see Claudette. He remembered that much. Gingerly, he felt his jaw. Swollen, throbbing, his heart beat so strong among the bruises. He ran his tongue around the inside of his mouth and thanked God he still had all of his teeth.

The thirst squeezed his throat in a clamp full of needles. It took him some time to swallow.

Looking around in the developing gloom, he took in his surroundings. Apart from the buzzard, he realised he was still on top of the hill. But that was the best news. Monroe had taken his boots and his gun.

And that was not the worst news.

Making his way down to the flat, he saw his horse was gone.

He crumpled in despair.

This was bad. Worse than bad. This was a death sentence.

CHAPTER ELEVEN

THE story, as told by Amelie, was bad. Very bad. Almost forty years had passed by, and the murder of Benjamin Mumford remained unsolved. The pub hotel changed hands many times since, but no one ever stayed for very long. The last owners left under something of a cloud. Talk of illicit affairs were rife, but the truth remained unclear, and nobody really cared anyway. That had been four years ago. And now the Cartwrights were the new owners.

Sarah felt numb. The horror that her home was the scene of a murder made her deeply uncomfortable. She shuddered involuntarily. Amelie gave a comforting squeeze of the wrist. "Don't worry, there are no stories of ghosts linked with the ghastly deed."

"Don't joke," Sarah said, not in the mood for brevity. "To think I've actually slept in that place without knowing!"

"Perhaps that's for the best? Imagine the nightmares."

"I hope," Sarah said cautiously, "there are no more gruesome stories concerning our lovely new hotel?"

"Not that I know of, but rest assured that if I can dig any up, you'll be the first to hear them."

"Oh, thank you! That will be a great source of comfort to me in the days to come."

The sound of their laughter dwindled into an awkward silence as both lost themselves in thought.

"I wish we had met in happier circumstances," said Amelie at last.

"I am certain it will end well. Mr Cole seems like a very dependable man."

"Oh, I am sure he is, but he is past his prime. Twenty years ago, I would have no worries, but those men who broke in here ..." She shuddered. "Animals. Savages. I'm not sure if Mr Cole has enough sand to bring them to justice."

"He must have been here when the hotel murder occurred?"

"No, he was working with the army back then. The War was in its last throes, so to speak. This town was nothing more than a sorry collection of broken-down old shacks. I remember the hotel being built in that atmosphere of hope and rejuvenation. I think everyone believed peace would bring us all enormous wealth and happiness." Amelie sighed. "How foolish we were."

"Even so, the hotel was built and the town grew."

"Yes. People were making their way out West once again. The south was ravaged, but out here where the War had hardly touched us, people gathered together to establish new communities and improve the old ones."

"I hope what we do to the hotel will do the town justice – we want to help bring renewed investment, support business, help develop the town into a place in which people are proud, a place where people will come to settle down and live."

Smiling, Amelie reached over and squeezed Sarah's hand. "I wish you every success."

"Thank you, and I wish for you to get your life back."

"I shall, when my sister is home safe and well."

A footfall made them both turn.

Ryan Stone stood in the doorway, his chest heavily bandaged, but a healthy sheen on his face.

"Mr Stone," shouted Amelie, jumping to her feet. "You'll catch your death of cold. What are you doing out of bed?"

She went to him, tenderly taking his arm, preparing to steer him back inside.

Stone gently, but firmly, pushed her hand away. "I'm fine, Miss Gower. Truly."

"Well, it's going to become chilly, Sheriff. I don't want you catching anything."

"Miss Gower." His tone was serious, causing both women to tense up. "I need to know."

"Know what?"

"What were those men after? To kill your servant, bust this place up, abduct your sister?"

Stepping back, Amelie slumped back down in her seat. "I don't know."

"You must!" He followed her, towering over her, face stern, hard. "What could you possibly have that they wanted?"

"I told you," she'd set her face forward to look out across the darkening plain, "I don't know."

"I think you do."

"Sheriff!" blurted Sarah, horrified. "How dare you insinuate that poor Amelie might be lying."

"It's all right, Sarah," the younger of the Gower sisters said.

"No, it's not, Amelie! Sheriff, you have no cause to accuse Amelie of—"

"I haven't accused her of anything, but there's something she's not telling us. I'm lucky to be alive, I know that, but if those men were willing to shoot me dead, and anyone else who got in their way, what they were after must be of real importance. Or value. *Think,* Miss Gower. Is there anything, no matter how insignificant it may seem, that they might have wanted?"

She shook her head, sniffed, and wiped away renewed tears with a silk handkerchief she took from her sleeve.

"Please, Miss Gower, I beseech you. If there is anything you can—"

Her head snapped around, a scowl of abject fury seizing her features. "I've told you, Sheriff, but ..." She drew in a huge breath. "I will sleep on it and tell you in the morning if anything comes to mind."

Grunting, Stone inclined his head slightly, gave a brief smile towards Sarah and turned away, saying, "That is all I ask for, Miss Gower. Goodnight."

The two women sat in silence, neither returning the young sheriff's leaving salutation.

CHAPTER TWELVE

DESPITE his exhaustion, the new day seemed to offer Monroe a little hope. Drenched in sweat, his body glistened slug-like. The night's exertions left him weakened. Time was the great healer, or at least that's how the saying went. For Monroe, waiting was something he had learned to accept. It had not always been a smooth process. Naturally impatient, eager to get on with things, waiting was wasting, as far as he was concerned. Locked in his torment, he felt a little assured that soon he would be able to get on with his life.

He blinked. The sun, warm and bright, brought him renewed energy, and he sat up. The others snored and groaned around him, relieved and secure. Monroe brought them feelings of security. That was his gift, his power. Even the woman, who he believed to be dead when he first came upon them, slept the sleep of the contented. Yes, this would be a good day, he mused.

Closing his eyes, images of the past night invaded his brain, scorching the back of his eyes with the vividness of the memory. An involuntary shudder seared through him. How could so much have happened in so short a span of time?

Knocking down Cole was easy enough. Stripping him of his gun and boots barely caused him to break sweat. Leaving him out in the open with no water and no means to get back to the sister's house meant the old scout would not survive out here. Heat exhaustion followed by crippling thirst. He'd crawl under a clump of sage, wither and die.

Perfect.

By the time a search party came, Monroe and the others would be far away. The old woman would tell them all they wanted to know, and then the riches would flow into their pockets.

Simple.

Except for the horse.

The damned horse would not comply. Cole's horse. A game animal, as soon as Monroe took a step in its direction, it reared up, wild, unpredictable. Making a grab for the reins merely caused it to kick out. And then it bolted, galloping off into the night before Monroe could do anything about it.

Cole must have trained it to react that way.

For some small compensation, Monroe kicked Cole's inert body a few times in the ribs.

He'd enjoyed that.

Releasing a long sigh, Monroe stood up. He needed coffee, so he crossed to the nearest sleeping bundle and roused the man with his boot.

Rolling over, angry, disorientated, still half-asleep, the man lashed out with both hands. They were large, calloused hands, the hands of a manual labourer or farmworker. Ramming his fists into his eyes, he rubbed away the last vestiges of sleep and yawned loudly. "What are you doing waking me up like that!"

"Get up, Constantine, and make me some coffee."

The huge man glared. "Make your own."

Monroe's voice, when he spoke again, held something. Menace. Enough to cause the man to consider his next move. Not used to intimidation, he sensed instinctively there was danger simmering just under the surface. He got to his feet. An inch taller than Monroe, he nevertheless cowered, eyes downcast. "Yeah, sure," he said and staggered across to the remnants of the previous night's campfire and seized the coffee pot. "I'll go swill it out down in the stream. It won't take long."

"Never mind about that," said Monroe, "just get the beans and make it."

The mention of the stream brought concern to Monroe. If Cole could find it, and of course he could, then he would regain sufficient strength to make it back. He cursed under his breath.

"What's that?" said Constantine, shovelling in the last of the beans into the pot.

"Nothing. Just hurry up."

Finding a suitable rock, Monroe slumped down onto it and considered the still sleeping woman. "She told you nothing?"

"Eh? Her?" Constantine shook his head. "Not a word. She's a tough old bird, I'll give her that much. Hemmings slapped her around a bit, but she wouldn't give up anything."

"And the deed box?"

"Empty, save for an old plan of the place. Could be useful, I guess."

"But no lawyer's papers, no deeds, no signed testimonials?"

"Is you deaf, Seb? I said it was *empty*." He looked around. "I need water. I'll have to fetch some."

"Light the fire first."

"Hell, black I may be, but I ain't your slave! We was freed, remember!"

Monroe studied the man's features, the broad nose, the skin that appeared so smooth, gleaming in the sun. Monroe had seen him with his shirt off, knew him to be a superb specimen of manhood, but his insolence riled him something awful. "Just do it!"

"And what you gonna do if I don't?"

In a blur, Monroe produced Cole's gun from his waistband, cocking the hammer and aiming it unerringly in one, smooth motion. "I'll kill yeh."

For a fleeting moment, it seemed Constantine might react, but then something dawned on him – the certainty of imminent death perhaps. His shoulders dropped, and he turned away.

Monroe shot him anyway, between the shoulder blades, and watched the big man fall face-first into the dirt.

Sighing, Monroe sat and waited for the rest of the camp to spring to life, which they did in a mess of flapping arms, high-pitched shrieks, and desperate clawing at firearms. Except for the woman, of course, who sat still as a stone, eyes boring into him as she spoke. "You're going straight to hell, you know that, don't you."

Monroe closed his eyes. Her expression troubled him, unlike her words, which made no impression on him whatsoever. "I've known that for a long time, ma'am."

"Well, I'm glad about that."

Monroe got up to retrieve the coffee-pot, ignoring his companions' screams and their pathetic attempts to revive the dead Constantine. Soon their garbled, excitable voices became nothing more than background noise, and at the trickle of a stream, he sat down, washed water over his face, and already knew the day had turned very bad indeed.

CHAPTER THIRTEEN

STONE wasn't sure what woke him, but he sat up, alert, and reached for his gun. Wincing as a stab of pain raced across his chest, he slowly rolled out of bed and stood up. Taking his time, calming his breathing, he padded to the open bedroom door and listened for a moment. There was nothing, so he went straight out onto the porch.

It was Cole's horse.

With painful but required slowness, Stone stepped down and moved up to the animal, conscious of the need not to make any sudden gestures. However, the horse appeared calm. Watchful, its eyes never left him as he tenderly reached out a hand and stroked its nose.

"Where's your master, eh?" he said softly.

He scanned the surroundings. There was no sign of Cole, and the fear gradually crawled up Stone's spine. The man who rode with him, the one Cole clearly had misgivings over, was missing also. Nothing about this seemed right.

Leading the horse to the rear of the spread, he entered the coolness of the barn. Working quickly but carefully, he removed the saddle and bridle and, despite his discomfort, wiped the horse down before fetching some oats. The water trough was within a few paces.

Drooping the saddle over the rail separating the stalls, Stone noted the empty Winchester scabbard. This definitely was not good.

He went outside again.

Amelie was there, still dressed in her nightdress, stretching out her arms. She smiled as Stone approached, a smile that faded as she saw the obvious stress he was under.

"Sheriff? What is going on?"

"It's Cole's horse," he said, stepping up beside her. "It must have made its way back here."

"But where is Mr Cole?"

Stone shrugged. "I don't know." He allowed his eyes to return to the vast expanse of open, daunting country. "Out there somewhere."

"Oh my Lord," she said. "You think something has happened to him?"

Stone nodded. "That's my guess."

"Something bad?"

"Who can say, but his horse wouldn't have returned here if everything was fine and dandy, that's for sure." A sudden resolve came into his features. "I'm going to go out and see if I can pick up his trail. I'll take Cole's horse, and I'll—"

"You can't," Amelie spurted. "Sheriff, for pity's sake, they've already tried to murder you – they won't fail the next time!"

"I'll be fine. I'll take it real careful, Miss Amelie, I promise."

"At least wait until Doctor Wycliffe returns – he said he would call to check up on your progress."

"Well, I'll wait an hour for Cole's horse to recover a little, but then I'll head on out. Where's Mrs Cartwright?"

"She returned to town after you'd fallen asleep. She too is going to return, with the good doctor, I shouldn't wonder."

"It's a pity none of them have a rifle I can use. I don't suppose you have one lying around someplace?"

"Old Joshua used to keep an old Enfield musket out in his bunkhouse."

"He has some cartridges?"

"I believe so. It's an old gun, so he used powder and lead shot to scare off the coyotes." Her eyes glazed over. "Poor Joshua, he was innocent in all of this. Who are these people, Sheriff?"

"You said you were gonna think on what I'd said, Miss Amelie – if there is anything you can think of that might have brought these men here?"

"I have thought, yes. There is something. The *only* thing. Come on inside, Sheriff. I'll fix you some breakfast and tell you what I know. I should have thought of it before, but what with the attack, Claudette's abduction, Joshua ... I hope it will help."

"It's understandable, Miss Amelie. All this upset, it's a wonder you recall anything at all."

"You're very gracious, Sheriff, but I fear my lapse of good sense may have put everyone in mortal danger."

She took him by the arm and led him inside.

CHAPTER FOURTEEN

COLE knew it was there, he could smell it, as well as hear it. Sometime in the night, he dragged himself to the stream and plunged face first into the cool water. The shocking cold exploded across his skin, revitalising him, and he wallowed in it, allowing himself as much time as he needed to restore strength and mobility to his aching bones.

Later, he slept.

The heat from the morning sun woke him. A further wash, more drinking, and he was on his feet, moving with stealth and speed, keeping the stream close. Soaked through to the skin, at first he shivered with the cold. Soon the heat made its mark, and within the hour, he was dry.

He followed the signs, wondering what had happened to his horse. Monroe must have taken him. He'd taken everything else. Tracking kept his mind focused, forced him to continue despite the throbbing in his jawline and the discomfort of his bare feet on the hard ground. With each step, the jolt caused him to wince. He constantly felt all across his face, searching for broken bones. He was lucky there were none.

The pain from his blistered, bleeding feet at last forced him to seek some shelter. From the position of the sun, he tried to calculate how long he'd been moving across the plain. Guessing it must have been no more than three hours, he found clumps of undergrowth by the stream and managed to fashion himself enough cover to shelter from the sun's glare.

He needed to wait until the air grew a little cooler.

Almost an entire day.

The coming night would bring intense cold, but it would be easier to travel. Not for the first time, he wondered if anyone would miss him. Stone perhaps? If the young sheriff was well enough, he could come out and search. Or, just as easily, he may decide to stay in bed.

Taking in shallow breaths, Cole did his best to rest. The heat sucked all energy from him, combining with his many bruises to make it virtually impossible to continue, even if he wanted to.

But he didn't, and instead, he slept.

At about the same time that Cole curled himself up under the meagre undergrowth, the Reverend Peters was leaving the backdoor of the small church annexe where he lived to begin his daily walk away from the town to the surrounding countryside. As he rounded the first bend before entering the twisting trail, he groaned inwardly when he saw one of his parishioners striding anxiously towards him. Usually, there were very few passers-by in this part of town. Those that he saw were not particularly interested in him. His congregation was small, mostly elderly, and few ventured beyond their front doors unless it was absolutely necessary. Seeing Mrs Jenkins was, therefore, something of a surprise. When she began waving at him furiously, it soon dawned on him that perhaps this day wasn't going to be so peaceful or as uninterrupted as he had hoped. A solitary, private man, he had few pleasures in life; one of them was keeping fit, and it was a pastime that was almost as rigorously pursued as his pastoral duties. He did, however, try to keep his interests well out of the public eye. He knew that his occasional visit to the local mercantile store to purchase his weekly bottle of whisky was frowned upon, but he had never been drunk, not in all the time he had taken his vows, so he could live with the unspoken criticism. But he did guard his other pleasures jealously. The idea of Mrs Jenkins accosting him during the week was one thing, but to see him in an open-necked shirt and work trousers would mean the whole town knowing his business before the day was out. It was a tedious, tiresome irritation that would mar his day.

"Mr Peters, I'm so glad it's you," Mrs Jenkins spurted, gripping his arm as he slowed down beside her.

Noting the woman's stark, worried face, Peters realised this was something more than the usual gossip he often found himself on the receiving end of. She was frightened. She needed him. His impatience, and annoyance if there had been any, disappeared, and he smiled, attempting to comfort her. It didn't work.

"There were three of them. I don't know who they were, but they were an uncouth bunch. I thought I recognised one of them, the biggest of the three, but I couldn't swear to it. I don't know where they are now, but you have to help."

Peters held the claw-like grip on his arm, as much to ease the pain as to reassure her. "Mrs Jenkins, just try and calm down."

"I will not calm down, Mr Peters," she rasped, her eyes flashing. "They were trying to get into my house! I was coming down the stairs when I heard them at my kitchen door. One of them was trying to prise it open with some sort of metal implement when I shouted at them. Mr Jenkins came down with his shotgun, and they ran off." She shuddered. "I hate to think what might have happened if he'd have shot them, but he wanted to, believe you me. They had smashed a window, no doubt to try and open the latch. That's what woke me, you see. Mr Jenkins said I should inform the Sheriff. I mean, it's unheard of here. Robbers and thieves are not something we have experienced, but of course, there is always a first time."

"Mrs Jenkins, please, just try and—"

"Well, we went outside. Mr Jenkins accompanied me just in case they were lurking close by. But, of course, when we reached the Sheriff's office, we discovered he was not there. And that dreadful Mr Cole, usually sitting and watching, he was absent as well. So, of course, you were my only choice, Reverend. My only choice."

"I understand Mr Cole went out to the Gower sisters' place. They'd reported seeing someone."

"Ah, well, there it is! The same gang, no doubt, forcing their way into people's homes, looking for valuables to rob. It's a disgrace, I tell you."

"But nothing was taken, was it? From your home, I mean?"

"Have you been listening to me?" Her face reddened. "I told you. Mr Jenkins chased them off."

"Yes, yes, and everything is all right, isn't it? Are you hurt?"

"I am not, thank the Lord. What would have happened if they had come in, over-powered my husband? Where would I be now? Lying in a pool of blood with no one to care two hoots."

"I doubt that, Mrs Jenkins, someone would have come."

"Who? Who would have come? Would you have come? Too interested in your daily strolls looking at the fields and the sky, daydreaming."

"Friends, neighbour," he said quickly, ignoring her jibes. "Somebody would have come."

"Nobody would have come, Reverend, nobody. Nobody cares. Nobody wants to get involved. I could be dead."

"Well, you're not dead, so we have that to be thankful for." He took a quick glance around. "Have you any idea where they went, in which direction?"

"None whatsoever. But I know what the one who had his hand on my door looked like. Big man. Blond hair, nasty looking, wearing a thin, blue jacket-thing."

Peters frowned. "Someone from the town, perhaps?"

"Folk from town keep themselves to themselves, Mr Peters. They're not thieves." She shook her head emphatically. "No, I'm certain they are not from round here. But the big one ... I've seen him before, I know it. But now they've got away. By the time the Sheriff decides to come back, they will be long gone. It's a disgrace he didn't leave a deputy in charge. That Matthias man isn't worth much and spends all his day sleeping. The town needs a proper law officer."

"Well, I think that's what Mr Cole was doing."

"That scoundrel? Dear Lord, he's worse than any of them. The things I've heard about him are enough to make one's toes curl!"

Peters held his breath. He too had heard the stories, but he did his best to ignore malicious talk. Cole struck him as an honourable man, a private person, but resourceful. Undoubtedly he had a past, but it was a past. It was the present that mattered, and Cole appeared a just person, despite never attending church. "Mrs Jenkins, if I may say so, you and your husband were a touch foolhardy to confront them the way you did."

She looked into his eyes, holding them for an icy moment. "We've no one else to protect us, Reverend," her words hissed out from between her teeth. "If we hadn't stood up to them, they'd be back, thinking that we are an easy target. Well, we're not. Frightened, yes, but you've got to show them that they can't win."

"I wish I had your courage."

She shook her head sadly. "So do I."

"Where is your husband now?"

"He's back home, replacing the glass in the window. When will the Sheriff be back?"

"I said I don't know. Soon I hope." A sudden thought struck him. "Mrs Jenkins, I will do what I can. I shall accompany you to your home, take some details and pass them on to Mr Cole on his return. Perhaps he and the Sheriff will then try and track them ..." It came to him then at a rush. "Oh my, Mrs Jenkins! I've just remembered."

"Remembered what?"

"Mr Cole. He went out to the Gower's place because something had happened. Miss Amelie, she spoke of it, and Cole set off there with another man – a *big* man, with blond hair."

"You can't possibly think ..." She allowed her voice to trail away as her hand came to her mouth. "But no, it must be a coincidence."

"Let us pray it is so, Mrs Jenkins."

"Reverend, if that man is the same, then something must have happened to Mr Cole. Something dreadful."

The Jenkins' home stood in a row of three at the end of a narrow lane leading off from the main street. It was pretty little place, white-painted walls with red-framed windows and an expensive slate roof. A wisteria trailed around the pillars supporting the porch canopy.

"The broken window is around back," explained Mrs Jenkins, opening the small gate which led into the tidy front garden. She led him along the path which circled the house.

The rear porch door hung open.

There was no sound from within.

"Henry?" she shouted, "Henry, I have brought the

Reverend Peters, and he wants to ..." The sound of her voice diminished as she disappeared inside.

Peters went to step in behind her and then froze as her scream pierced the still, morning air.

Recovering quickly, he rushed inside and found her standing rigid in the kitchen, hands bunched across her mouth, staring at what she found.

He followed her gaze and felt his knees go weak.

The place was a mess, cupboards torn open and contents thrown across the floor. And in the midst of it all lay Mr Jenkins.

Dead.

CHAPTER FIFTEEN

COLE sat up, senses on high alert. Unconsciously he reached for his Colt Cavalry and cursed when he remembered Monroe had taken it. So he sat, listening, ready to make a bolt for it if needed.

Two horses, approaching a little way off. Cole's highly developed skills did not desert him at that moment. The sound the horses made were distinctive. Only one bore a rider.

He quickly looked about him. There were numerous rocks, twigs, but nothing big enough to use as a weapon. Then he saw something, a branch lying half-submerged in the gently flowing stream. Stripped of bark, it glowed ivory white under the water. Reaching out, he took it, hefting it in his hands. It would suffice.

Moving quietly, he edged away from the stream. Always looking, always ready, Cole slinked forward, a predator, silent as the night.

The rider drew closer.

Cole could smell the horse sweat.

Only one rider. It would be easy enough.

He burst from his cover, crying out, hands held aloft, the makeshift club he'd found ready to smash down onto the rider.

Taken by surprise, the lead horse reared up, terrified. Battling gamely, the rider clung on while behind him the second, riderless horse kicked and bucked in its desperation to get away.

Cole stopped, recognising both animals and the man.

Quickly, he grabbed hold of the lead horse's reins and struggled to bring it under control. It fought fiercely, alive with terror, its flanks heaving, front legs lashing out. Gritting his teeth, muscles straining, Cole held on, soothing the wretched animal with soft, soothing reassurance. Eventually, with a good deal of gentle coercion, Cole managed at last to calm it. Behind, the other horse seemed to know instinctively what was happening. As its eyes settled on Cole, a sudden change overcame it. Instantly fear was replaced with relief, body relaxing, and it nudged forward, pressing its head into Cole's chest. Laughing, Cole held it with both arms and breathed, "My darling, all is well."

"Cole?"

Cole turned in the direction of the voice and saw Stone, calming his own horse, gawping at him in total astonishment.

"Cole, what in the name of Hades are you doing here?" He jumped down and embraced the old scout warmly in his arms. "I thought you were a goner for sure."

"So did I, Ryan. So did I!"

Stone's face grew serious. "Mr Cole, you don't look so good."

"I took a fearful beating, Ryan, and I was a fool not to be ready for it."

"Who was it?"

"The big fella I recruited to help. Monroe, he calls himself, but whether or not that's his real name, I couldn't tell you. He's in cahoots with the men who attacked Claudette Gower, and I suspect he was hanging around the town to cook up some plan or other."

"Plan? What sort of plan?"

Stroking his horse's neck, Cole gingerly put his bare foot into the stirrup and grimaced. "He took my boots as well as my gun, but I'll repay him." Gritting his teeth, he hauled himself into the saddle and leaned forward to soothe the horse again. "Yes," he said, flicking the reins and easing the horse around in a tight circle, "I reckon they are planning something. Not sure what, but it has something to do with what went down at the Gower's place."

"I agree it is strange, to attack Claudette the way they did, shoot down poor Joshua. But Amelie told me some things, Mr Cole, information that just might solve this mystery." He mounted his horse and moved alongside the old former scout. "I reckon we head back to town, fix you up, and put our heads together in order to plan what to do next."

"Amelie is back in the cabin?"

"Yes, she is."

"I'm not sure it's wise to leave her there all alone. We'll head back there first, then we'll all go back into town."

Nodding in agreement, Stone set his jaw, kicked his horse into a gallop, and before long, both men were making short work of the journey back to Amelie Gower.

CHAPTER SIXTEEN

SARAH lay in bed staring at the ceiling, making patterns with the cracks, her imagination creating a host of pictures. It was late, but she didn't care. She could hear Lewis downstairs, lugging bits of furniture around, grunting, groaning, sometimes singing tunelessly. She envied his positive outlook. For her, the initial thrill of the arrival was soon replaced by anxiety. They'd taken on too much, she knew it.

Rolling over, she gazed out of the window. Another beautiful day. Against the advice of close friends, she had agreed to come here, doing her best to support her husband. Lewis was a good man. Weak, ineffective in so many ways, he nevertheless wanted to make them a good life, and he believed the hotel would give them that. But they had to make it work. Already Sarah had witnessed first-hand what this area was like. The promise of violence forever lurking in the darkened corners. And the story of what happened in the cellar. She shuddered, threw back the bedclothes, and stood up.

Padding downstairs, she came across Lewis as he emerged from the dining room, sleeves rolled up, lathered in sweat.

"You could do with a drink," she said. He answered with a slight smile and moved behind the bar.

"I haven't fitted any casks," he said. "Not sure who the supplier will be."

"We have some bottles." She opened one and poured him a beer. She watched him drink it. "I went with Amelie to her cabin. The Sheriff is well on the way to recovery."

"Glad to hear it."

"That Mr Cole went off with some brutish-looking character to try to track down the killers."

Lewis jerked the bottle from his lips. "Killers?"

"Don't you pay attention to anything? Where have you been, Lewis?"

"Here, working."

"Well, I have learned a spicy story to do with this place."

"Don't tell me," breathed Lewis with a sigh, putting down the finished bottle and wiping his hands on a bar towel, "let me guess. There was a gruesome murder committed here some years ago. The body was found in our cellar, but the culprit – or culprits – have never been found. Am I warm?"

"You horrible man!" Laughing, she seized the bar-towel and threw it at him. "How did you know all that?"

"Reverend Peters told me."

"The Reverend?"

"Yes. He's a strange one. Did you notice his hands?"

Another laugh. "I noticed his body."

"I thought you might," he grinned.

"Who wouldn't? He's nothing like you'd expect a man of the cloth to look like."

"I guess not. You'd expect a reverend to be all pink and wobbly, not built like a brick outhouse." Lewis shook his head thoughtfully. "There's more to him than he wants us to know. I noticed his hands. Hard hands, gnarled. Been in a fight or two, I'd say."

"You noticed a lot."

"Couldn't help it. He came in while you were out,

helped me move quite a few things. He reminded me of someone I met back in Kansas. He had that same sort of *something*. I don't know, an aura. People said he was a prize-fighter."

"You think that's what the Reverend is? Sounds a bit far-fetched, Lewis. A man of the church?" She shook her head. "Perhaps he just keeps himself in good shape. Nothing sinister in that."

"Perhaps not."

They both flinched at the first scream.

Already, Sarah was moving from behind the counter, Lewis close behind.

Stepping outside, they both saw a woman staggering down the main street, overtaken by a sprinting man.

A large man, racing towards the Sheriff's office.

"Oh my Lord," breathed Sarah.

The big man was the Reverend Peters.

CHAPTER SEVENTEEN

OLD man Grimes pushed his way through the murmuring crowd when he saw the horses approaching. He waved them down.

"What's going on, Larry?" asked Stone.

Grimes held onto the Sheriff's reins as Stone dismounted.

"There's been a killing. Matthias has the witnesses inside."

Cole, sporting a pair of old Joshua's boots, jumped down and immediately regretted it. He clutched at his side. "Who?"

"Mr Jenkins. His wife and the Reverend discovered him. Seems like a gang broke into the house and killed him stone dead. Mrs Jenkins, she's in a terrible state. Doc Wycliffe gave her a sedative, but Miss Gower is with her right now."

"Thanks for that, Larry," said Stone and shot a glance towards Cole. "You reckon it's the same gang?"

"Almost certainly."

"But why break into the Jenkins' place?"

"That is indeed the question," said Cole.

"Mrs Jenkins said they tried to break in earlier," said Larry, "but Mr Jenkins ran 'em off."

"Did she see them?" asked Stone hopefully.

"Not sure. She and the Reverend came racing across here in a real state, rousing the whole town. Poor old Matthias didn't know what to do. They're all inside."

Cole sighed. "Larry, I need a new gun."

Grimes frowned. "Oh. I don't think I have anything like your Colt, Mr Cole, but I have some revolvers."

"As long as it shoots straight, I don't care what it is."

The chosen gun did indeed shoot straight. Similar to the revolver Sterling Roose carried, it was a Smith and Wesson Model 10 with a six-inch barrel. Cole liked it for two reasons – one, because it reminded him of his old friend and two; perhaps more importantly, it was double-action.

He took it out back and practised for a while. Satisfied, he bought the gun and holster together with enough ammunition for what he had in mind.

Returning to the Sheriff's office, with the crowd still pressing forward trying to get a view of what was happening, he began to force his way through to get inside.

"Oh, Mr Cole," said a voice.

He turned to see Sarah Cartwright and her husband standing there, both ashen-faced.

"Dear Lord," said Lewis Cartwright in shocked tones. "What on earth happened to you?"

Running his fingers lightly over his bruised face, Cole shrugged. "A slight altercation. What is going on here?"

"That's what we're trying to find out," said Sarah. "I'm very worried for Amelie, who is in there with the Reverend and Mrs Jenkins."

"We think it's more killings," said Lewis. Those close by gave out a collective gasp of shock.

Not wanting to speculate, Cole merely nodded, then continued squeezing through to the door. He pounded on it, shouting out who he was. He heard the bolt drawn back, and he stepped inside. The old deputy, Matthias Thurst, beckoned him forward.

Immediately on seeing Cole, the Reverend Peters stood and thrust out his hand. "Mr Cole, it's a pleasure seeing you so well."

Cole smirked. "Not sure if that's particularly true, Reverend," he said, only too aware of the reaction his swollen jawline brought, "but thank you anyway."

Matthias closed and bolted the door.

Amelie Gower, sitting next to Mrs Jenkins, comforting her, turned a hopeful face towards the former scout. "Anything?"

He turned his face away, not knowing what to say. "Not yet, Miss Amelie. Try not to be too alarmed. We will get 'em, and, I assure you, we will rescue your sister."

"Mr Cole," said Stone, stepping forward and handing the former scout one of the Winchesters he kept in a rack behind his desk, "the good Reverend has managed to extract a description of the perpetrators from Mrs Jenkins."

"The one doing all the shouting was a large, blond man," said Amelie Gower, putting her arm around the older lady to comfort her. "She's in a dreadful state, Mr Cole."

"I can see, ma'am." Cole's tone was grave. He blew out a long sigh as he checked the Winchester. "All right, I'll see what tracks and signs I can find at the Jenkins' house. We'll need men, Ryan. Last time I tried to gather together a posse, I didn't have much success. That was probably down to Monroe intimidating everyone."

"I'm willing to help," said the Reverend.

Cole considered him for a long time. He certainly looked the part, a man of considerable physical advantages. "Can you shoot?"

"If needed."

"I think we can all say it'll be needed, Padre."

"Reverend is just fine, Mr Cole."

"As you wish."

"Mr Cole," said Stone, "I have to remind you, this isn't the Wild West any longer. We have laws now, very strict they are too. We can't just go riding out into the Badlands and gun them down."

"Don't see why not."

"This is what I mean," said Stone, growing uncomfortable. "We have to follow due process. We need to find them and arrest them."

"And if they resist? Ryan, these men are killers. They are clearly after something and will stop at nothing to get it. Whatever it is."

"Perhaps it is all to do with the murder?" All eyes turned to the Reverend. "At the hotel, I mean. We all know it happened, but none of us know the details."

"I do," said Mrs Jenkins in a low voice.

"Now, you just stay quiet, Mrs Jenkins," said Amelie soothingly. "There is no need to get yourself all upset over any of this. No more than you already are."

"No, it needs to be said. I told that new owner, Mrs Cartwright. I told her everything."

Stone cleared his throat, lowering his voice, as respectful as he could be when he said, "And how come you know it all, Mrs Jenkins?"

"My husband." A tiny shudder. Amelie squeezed her hand. Mrs Jenkins smiled. "I'm all right. My husband was a lawyer, retired, of course. He was in charge of the original sale nigh-on forty years ago. His brother-in-law bought the hotel. I was never happy with any of it. He was a detestable man, but my husband assured me everything was legal."

"But why would these men ..." Stone's voice became pained. "I'm sorry, Mrs Jenkins, but why would these men murder your husband because of something that happened forty years ago?"

"Perhaps if I told you the story, together we might be able to make some sense of it?"

So, as the others sat down and Cole pulled up a chair to do the same, Mrs Jenkins told the story of what happened in the Elegance Hotel all that time ago.

CHAPTER EIGHTEEN

Mumford was his name. He took over the running of the hotel around forty years ago. It was he who christened it "The Elegance," although why nobody knew because it was a squalid looking place, with chipped paint and warped boarding.

The evening it happened, he was closing the bar. Having dismissed Mrs Taylor, the receptionist, a half-hour before, he was alone. Business had been slack recently, and he saw no point in paying good wages for her to simply sit around.

Wheezing, he lifted the hatch to the cellar and climbed down the few damp, dark steps that led into the gloom. He picked one of the torches he always kept down there and lit it. Tinder dry, it flared violently, allowing him a good view of the surroundings. The place stank. He rarely came down here nowadays. Since his wife had left him, there was no one to badger him over keeping the place tidy. Even so, he needed some timber to repair a creaking card table in the lounge, so he set to gathering together several small planks from the stack in the far corner.

Mumford was not a well man. The dank air, combined with particles of dust, had got on his chest, and he was having some difficulty in breathing. He moved away, wheezing painfully now, and decided to take some fresh air before he re-

sumed his work. He blew his nose loudly and placed his foot on the first step, ready to go back up into the bar area.

The kick took him full in the face, tearing his nostrils and upper lip with the force of the blow. He careened backwards, the pain and shock not yet hitting him. As he smashed into assorted crates and barrels, he had the vaguest impression that an army of bodies was charging towards him through the gloom. He screamed, not really sure who or what his attackers were, conscious only of the searing pain wincing through his heavily bleeding face.

He floundered across the dusty floor, his left hand raised in a pathetic attempt to ward off anymore blows, whilst his right hand supported his half-prostrate and trembling body. The blood dripped unchecked from his shattered nose and mouth, and he watched in fascination as it splashed onto the ground.

A dark shape loomed over him, and Mumford at last found the ability to speak. No sooner did his mouth form the first syllable than it was filled with something he did not at first recognize. It was like a blow from a slab of cold, hard metal, so powerful was its delivery. His mind whirled in disarray, and, unable to concentrate properly, he felt like a helpless, foolish drunkard. Nothing was making sense.

Suddenly hands were lifting him up again, propping him against what was left of the stack of barrels. He sat, head on chest, blinking through the tears, watching the blood spreading over his shirt as it dripped from his face, waiting in total helplessness for the next onslaught.

There was silence.

Mumford, at last given the opportunity to think logically, wondered who in the name of God was doing this to him, and why. If it was burglars, why such violence – they could have easily locked the cellar door on him and then ransacked the hotel at their leisure? It was nonsensical and so unnecessary – not a brave man, he would have willingly given them whatever they wanted without any struggle at all.

Distorted images flashed across his consciousness. From somewhere, he found the strength, and courage, to raise his head. A weak, shaking hand moved across his eyes, smearing away the blood and tears that marred his vision. He managed to make out the form of his attacker. He sat opposite, staring in silence, casually filling a bone pipe with tobacco. Mumford marvelled at his audacity and great strength. He was a lone attacker. To lift someone of Mumford's weight would demand an enormous effort, and this man had done it with seeming ease. The realization that here was someone who could destroy him utterly and totally sent new shock waves of horror through Mumford's already battered and defeated body. He could do nothing to defend himself against such an individual, and the knowledge disturbed him greatly.

A match blazed briefly in the gloom, and Mumford caught a glimpse of the man's face. The shock of recognition caused him to involuntarily jerk his head back, a rasp of breath hissing through his chipped teeth.

"Morgan!"

The name was like a slap to the man. He came closer, the pipe clamped in the corner of his hard, handsome face, the lips pulled back in a sneer. "Hello, Mumford," he said, propping one foot next to the innkeeper. "Where's Nancy?"

Mumford recoiled as a stream of smoke was blown into his face. Turning away, he coughed hoarsely. His breathing gargled in his chest.

The face came closer, the words like blows. "I asked you a question!"

Mumford had no idea where his wife was. "She left, a few days ago."

"Is that a fact?" Morgan stepped back, his eyes quickly scanning the eerie half-light of the cellar. Stooping down, he picked up one of the pieces of wood Mumford had chosen to repair the card table. He weighed it in his hand, then advanced on his victim. "You see, she told me she was only leaving for a short time, to teach you a lesson. She said she was going back to you."

"I don't understand. To teach me a lesson? I thought you and she were—"

"We had a tiff. Silly girl found me in bed with..." He smiled broadly. "Well, let's just say she wasn't too happy about it." He let out a long stream of pipe smoke. "Funny things women, don't you think?"

Mumford said nothing. He was concentrating on his breathing, which was becoming a little easier. He looked up into Morgan's maniacal face, the face of a man capable of anything. "You must know she wouldn't come back to me," he managed to say through his already swollen lips.

Morgan looked impressed, but for other reasons. "You mean because I'm a much better lover than you? So much better that she couldn't bear to think of sharing your bed after having shared mine?"

Mumford nodded his head meekly. "Yes."

"I'm glad you've accepted the truth, at long last."

"I always knew she wanted you more than me."

"Really? That's very gracious of you." He pressed his face closer still to Mumford's. "Tell me why you think that's so?"

Mumford swallowed hard. He could smell the man's smoky breath, feel the sweat of his face, sense the insanity that was bubbling just under the surface. But he could also sense that the man's ego was perhaps the most dangerous thing to contend with. If he could keep that sweet then perhaps Mumford could find a way out of this ghastly mess. "Because you are a better man than me," he gushed, guessing it was what Morgan wanted to hear.

Morgan's voice rose in triumph. "Yes! Yes, I am." He stepped back, looking for all the world like a strutting peacock.

The situation was still dangerous, Mumford well aware that only total submission could possibly prevent further violence.

"Tell me more. Tell me how I'm stronger and cleverer than you, that Nancy can't resist me, yearns for me, begs for me to be with her. Tell me all of that."

Mumford did, repeating every word.

Morgan cackled in victory. "You're in awe of me, aren't you? You wish you were like me."

"*Yes, yes, I do.*"

"*But you never will be. Never.*"

From the foot of the stairs, taking both men by surprise, a voice cracked through the fetid air. "You're an embarrassment!"

Mumford stared. Nancy Mumford stood at the foot of the cellar steps wearing a delicately patterned summer dress of powder blue.

"Hello, Nancy," said Morgan.

Mumford took his chance whilst Morgan's attention was diverted. It was desperate, and probably futile, but his only hope. He launched himself forwards, slamming the whole of his considerable weight into the Morgan's midriff, and both of them crashed to the ground.

Morgan's strength proved too much, and he easily disentangled himself, lifted Mumford to his feet, and slammed his knee into Mumford's groin. Mumford yelped and sagged in Morgan's strong hands before a heavy left swung through the air and cracked into his jaw, felling him. Whimpering as he writhed on the ground, Mumford blubbered and begged Nancy to call the sheriff.

But Nancy didn't move. She watched, mesmerised, as Morgan picked her husband up, threw him against the far wall, and used one of the wooden planks to break open Mumford's skull as if it were an egg. She saw, but could not believe, the glint of steel as a long-bladed knife appeared in Morgan's hand. He sliced through Mumford's ponderous belly effortlessly, gutting him like a pig, the contents tumbling out in a gush of blood and gore.

Nancy stared, watching speechless with disbelief.

When it was done and the blood-spattered corpse lay butchered amongst the wreckage of the crates, Morgan stood, limp-wristed, gazing at the consequences, gulping in air, but face blank and impassive, registering nothing.

Waking as if from a dream, Nancy moved to his shoulder and tentatively pulled at his jacket, taking care that no blood splattered onto her. She felt a curious thrill buzzing through her. Although the scene had been horrific, she had marvelled at Morgan's skill and strength, and she now felt elated that this man was hers.

Morgan turned to her. "Bit of a mess," he said quietly, almost in a whisper. Nancy looked deep into his eyes and could find no remorse, fear, or anything else there. "We'd better get the deeds and go," she said.

"Go where?" said Morgan, regaining some of his confidence. "We can't go anywhere that's far enough away. I'm finished."

"No, you're not," she snapped, her resolve hardening. "We can get out of this. No-one knows you're here, and I'm the only witness and," a smile crossed her lovely mouth, "I didn't see a thing."

He went to hold her, but she stopped him with an upturned hand. "Sorry," he said, realizing the blood was all over his shirt front.

"We'll get you a change of clothes, get the deeds, make the claim, and then work out how we can rebuild our lives."

"But what about this," he gestured, without looking, at Mumford's corpse. "Somebody's sure to come along and discover him, and then they'll launch a manhunt."

"And who will they look for? You? Me? Why?" She shook her head. "I'll report it, include a few half-truths and tell the sheriff I left but came back out of guilt; that I found him like this, the victim of a terrible robbery gone wrong. We're going to be all right, I promise you."

He was shaking his head. "But the claim. As soon as you cash it, they'll put two and two together."

"No, I'll put the hotel up for sale, lie low. We've waited this long, we can wait a little longer. When everything is calm, we'll meet up and get away." She stroked his face. "You're everything he wasn't. We've done the hard part, now we just need to stay calm." She leaned forward, careful of the blood, and kissed him lightly on the lips. "I like your arrogance. I like that a lot, but most of all I like your confidence. I like you, or didn't you know that?"

"Nothing more than like?"

She smiled, all thoughts of the nightmare vision she had just witnessed gone from her mind. They were a well-matched pair. "Anything more will come later. Come on, let's get you some clothes..."

CHAPTER NINETEEN

"I told much the same story to Lewis Cartwright," said the Reverend Peters as the others sat in silence, digesting what Mrs Jenkins had told them.

"And how did he react?" asked Stone.

"To be honest, he didn't react at all."

"As if he knew it already?"

"Perhaps, but I don't see how he could have."

"The story is well-known," said Mrs Jenkins. "They tracked them both down, eventually. Silas Morgan was killed in a gunfight, and Nancy Mumford arrested. She made a full statement before her trial. Every gruesome detail was included. Although she wasn't directly responsible for the killing of her husband, a lot of people hated her for her involvement with Morgan and they hanged her."

Stone threw out his hands, exasperated. "And the business about the deeds? What happened to the deeds?"

No one offered any explanation, Mrs Jenkins alone added, "My husband had something to do with it. I think they might have been put into some sort of trust, for Nancy Mumford's grandchildren, but I can't be sure, and of course, now, we can't ask him." Shaking her head, she pressed her handkerchief into her eyes and wept, Amelie holding her tightly around the shoulders.

Stone stood up. "Mr Cole, if you could be so kind as to get the horses ready, I shall wander down to talk to Mr Cartwright in the meantime."

Cole arched a single eyebrow, and he asked, "Something troubling you?"

"Not sure. There's a lot not right about any of this. With what we know, it's almost as if the hotel is the key."

"The hotel?" Peters said, shaking his head. "How can a building be the cause of murder?"

"Well, it already is a place where a murder took place," said Stone. "What happened there forty years ago has some bearing on what is going on here right now. I'm sure of it."

Doffing his hat, Stone made his apologies to the ladies and left. Cole studied the two women, noting their strained faces. He stood up. "Reverend, I'm riding over to my home. I need to explain to Maddie what's going on. She's probably worried sick."

"All right," said Peters. He picked up one of the Winchesters from Sheriff Stone's desk and weighed it in his hands. "Been a while since I've handled one of these." He looked up to see Cole's inquiring glance. "I wasn't always a preacher, Mr Cole."

"You served in the Army?"

Peters inclined his head, thoughtful and quiet. Cole sensed there was a small touch of shame when he again spoke, "Yes. I served in the Spanish-American War. Fought in Cuba and was to be shipped across to the Philippines when I got shot in the calf." He patted his right leg. "I was invalided out." He shook his head. "That was a vicious war, Mr Cole, I don't mind telling you. A lot of things done that shouldn't have been. I spent a lot of soul-searching afterwards as I lay in a hospital bed and decided I wanted to do something of good, if you understand me. So, I joined the clergy. Methodist minister is what I am, although many around here don't seem to care what I am as long as it isn't them standing in the pulpit."

"I wouldn't know. I'm not one for church-going myself."

"Well, after what I saw in that war, I'm not so certain if many people are." He worked the Winchester lever. "I'll wander out back and shoot off a few rounds."

After he'd left, the atmosphere lightened appreciably. Mrs Jenkins was the first to speak. "I knew there was something about him. He's ... Well, he's very *physical*. I saw him change when we ..." Her head fell, and she sniffed loudly. "When we went back to the house and saw—"

"It's all right," said Amelie. "You don't need to say anymore."

"No, no, I'm fine. But the Reverend, he became quite angry. Muttering all sorts of quite awful things and clenching his fists as if he meant to hit somebody."

Cole didn't say anything, gave a half-smile, and went outside. Deep in thought, he mounted his horse and gently edged it out of town, making his way to his home and Maddie.

CHAPTER TWENTY

HIS aim proved good. After emptying seven rounds into a makeshift target crafted out of an old, rotting piece of tree-trunk, Peters wiped his brow with his sleeve and sighed. His anger boiled. To have killed Mr Jenkins the way they did, then leaving the body so that his wife would find him. Obviously, it was meant as a warning. But why? It had been some time since Peters had experienced such wanton disregard for human life. This latest killing brought it all back.

He wandered through the back streets and entered the saloon by the rear entrance. There was a smattering of customers, but most people seemed to be on the street, wondering what was going on at the Sheriff's office. That suited Peters just fine, and he went to the bar and ordered a whisky. The barman gave him a look, which Peters returned, staring him down.

After the third drink, Peters began to come back to Earth. It took him some time to come to terms with the enormity of what he was capable of. Mr Jenkins' murder conjured up the demons he had kept buried for so long. Changing his direction, living a new life as a preacher, he'd managed to wipe away the memory of what it was like to experience pain. Suffering was a trite word to use; it didn't really say enough. Yes, he was suffering; yes, he *had* suffered; this was something more. He could taste it in his mouth. The bittersweet tang of wanting to punish. He knew it was wrong. He was weak, a failure. Failure in himself, his vows, his Lord. His shame was tangible, and it seeped from the very pores of his soul to mingle with the heavy atmosphere of that lonely saloon that warm summer's day.

Heavy shoulders stooped forward, the slow, deliberate movement of the hand to mouth as he drained the alcohol from the glass. If anyone watched, nobody had any idea that what they were witnessing was the torment of a man of God who had betrayed a promise he had made to himself long ago. The memory of those past times consumed him, and even the drink could not dull the vivid pictures that played across his mind.

In the searing midday heat, the patrol passed down the crumbling street, broken adobe buildings pressing in on both sides, dark faces peering out from within. Some way ahead, an upturned cart with two men furiously exchanging words. Suddenly alert, the soldiers brought up their rifles, fanning out in a thin line.

Peters, young and heavily muscled, had earned his corporal stripes under the heat of the Cuban sun. He recognised something amiss. He had grown old in that place, had visited the bowels of hell more than once, and had moulded himself into a vicious, professional killer, silent and resourceful. These streets had numbed his powers somewhat, but not enough for him to miss the tension that now hung in the atmosphere and was heavier than the warm air itself.

"Shepherd!"

A big lance-corporal turned and gave Peters an inquiring glance. "What's up, Corporal?"

"I don't know," Peters said, working the lever of his Winchester. "Take two others and go and check 'em out. And be careful, all right?"

Shepherd shrugged, called two soldiers over to him, and continued walking towards the two arguing men.

Hill and Stowell ambled alongside. It was too hot for all this.

A yelp of Spanish gave them all a start, forcing them all to reach for their weapons. It was only a boy, stepping out from between houses. They all gave a collective sigh of relief. Dressed in white, his shock of blue-black hair made a stark contrast to the brightness of his garb. He had a cheery, open face, his massive brown eyes like saucers, dispelling all mistrust.

From where he stood, Peters watched transfixed. He saw Shepherd's smile. The boy had an orange in his hand. It was a very big orange. Three more boys, all about the same age standing a little way back, were jabbering to each other. Remarkable how they all looked so similar, small, wiry, burned nutmeg brown by the sun.

Motioning for the other two to move forward, Shepherd tilted his head towards the boy. Peters turned to watching the streets. The quietness was intense.

The boy stepped closer with the orange, holding it out. "Cut, please," he was saying in English. Shepherd smiled again, slung his rifle over his shoulder, and reached for the knife at his belt.

The boy was close now. Thirteen years old at most, Peters calculated, intrigued by the little scene playing out some twenty or so paces from him. The boy seemed small for his age, undernourished, Peters mused, as so many were.

The boy continued to hold out the fruit for Shepherd to take and begin to peel. He was so tiny compared to Shepherd bearing over him. The lance-corporal bent forward and reached out with his free hand.

From where Peters stood, the whole incident fell into slow-motion. His eyes glazed over, and he felt himself spinning out of control as each minuscule event combined to present before him a scene from his worst nightmare. Time stood still; his body froze. His training, for a few brief and crucial moments, deserted him, and he could do little more than watch.

The boy was fast, faster than anything any of them had ever seen. The knife was like a blue streak, flashing brightly in the daylight, thrusting upwards, ripping into Shepherd's midriff, slicing upwards through his abdomen to his breast bone. Shepherd didn't scream, couldn't scream, the surprise was too great. As his mouth gaped open, he folded forward, holding onto the awful, open wound. The knife flashed again, back and across, the sharp blade slashing across the lance-corporal's throat. The blood spilled, and Shepherd fell.

Hill and Stowell moved, rifles turning, but they turned the wrong way, towards the boy. The two arguing Arabs were arguing no longer. From under their voluminous robes, the ancient pistols spat out a cruel blast of concentrated fire, and the two soldiers died in a hail of ill-aimed but highly effective lead shot.

The firing proved too inaccurate. As the soldiers died, so too did Shepherd's killer, the boy's little body racked by the two old Remingtons. There was another effect too: Peters.

Triggered by the violence, his training kicked in. Already he was rolling across the soft dust that seemed to lie everywhere. Kneeling behind what little cover there was, the Winchester Model 1892 proved highly effective in the big Corporal's hands. The two Cuban men met their deaths before they really knew what was happening. But Peters wasn't finished.

Out of control, thinking clouded by the horror he had witnessed, he strode from behind his cover, working the Winchester lever. The remaining boys reacted too slowly, and even before they were turning, Peters emptied his rifle into them, not caring if they were part of the ambush or innocent bystanders.

Silence settled. Peters stood rock still and watched his victims die.

As the mist before his eyes parted, reality slowly returned, and the enormity of what he had done sank home. The Winchester fell from trembling fingers, all thoughts of his safety gone. The heat, the blood, the scent of death, it was too much. Collapsing into the dirt, his head pressing against the sand, the stillness enveloped him. Overwhelmed by the senseless waste of life, and his shameful part in it, nothing could ever wipe away the image of those boys' faces. Nothing.

At the bar, Peters pushed away the memories and considered his glass. The past had caught up with him at last, the violence he had rejected, the violence he had striven so hard to conceal, to control, to conquer, had risen up and taken hold of him once more. He hadn't changed at all. He still had the capacity to destroy. In Cuba, it had been with guns, guns he continued to know how to use. He had hidden behind his vows, struggling for respectability in what he stood for. It all seemed for nothing.

Blowing out a loud sigh, Peters snatched up the Winchester propped up beside him and wandered outside. Several townsfolk wandered by, giving him curious looks. He wondered if his attitude gave away his drinking bout, but he doubted it. He could still hold his liquor. No, they were probably more curious about his emerging from the saloon. A man of the cloth, and a Methodist at that, did not sit well with any sort of drinking establishment. But Peters was past caring. The murder of Mr Jenkins had brought it all back. The anger at man's inhumanity to man. And the shame over what he'd done. After this, he decided, he would leave the clergy, leave this town, seek out some other means of employment. One that did not require him speaking with people. He needed to escape, start over.

He contemplated the street. Sheriff Stone had mentioned something about talking with Lewis Cartwright, so he decided to go and discover for himself if any developments had been unearthed.

CHAPTER TWENTY-ONE

HELPING him take off his shirt, Maddie screwed up her mouth and groaned when she saw the large bruises across Cole's ribs.

"Don't fuss none," he said through gritted teeth. He moved awkwardly; the kicks he'd received had done damage. He didn't know how much.

"You need to see Doc Evans."

"Doc Evans is dead."

Her hand flew to her mouth. "Oh my Lord, since when?"

"Since about nine months ago." He shook his head but couldn't resist smiling. "Have you been living in a cave, or what?"

She went to punch him light-heartedly, as she usually did in reply to his sarcasm, but stopped herself just in time. "Who's his replacement? I mean, is there one?"

"Yes. Wycliffe. He seems a good man." He tried to stretch out his back, only succeeding in buckling himself up with pain.

"I'll run you a hot bath," Maddie said quickly. "You need to take it easy for a while."

"I can't," he said, sitting down and pulling off his boots. "There's been a killing over in town. I have to try and track them that did it down."

"*What*? Are you crazy? After what happened with that awful man, Soloman and poor Sterling? Reuben, you can't keep doing this! You told me you was retired, that Sterling's death had made you see that time had caught up with you, that you couldn't keep—"

"Maddie, please," he said, holding up both hands in surrender. "I know what I said, but it got complicated. Ryan was shot, and whilst he was recuperating, I sort of—"

"I don't care about Ryan, I care about *you*!"

"Hell, Maddie, he saved my life."

"So, what is this, a debt to be honoured? You're going to get yourself killed."

"No, I ain't."

"Yes, you are – look at you! You're all busted up."

Cole took a breath. He knew she was right, there was no point in trying to deny any of it. His body was telling him with every passing day that even the most menial of tasks caused him enormous effort. "He took me by surprise is all."

She gaped at him, incredulous. "Took you by surprise?" She ran a hand through her hair and Cole could help notice that it was shaking. The fight left her voice, resigned to his stubbornness. "Well, if that isn't a sign that you're too old for this, Reuben, I don't know what is."

"This is the last time, I swear it."

"You've said that before."

"I know, but Maddie, damn it all, I have no choice."

"You have every choice, you stubborn old fool."

She flounced off, leaving him sitting in the armchair, staring into nothingness. "*Old?*" he muttered to himself. "I'm sixty-two, so yes, I'm old…" He sat back, listening to her running the bath, and realised just how lucky he was. She was right, he knew it. Twenty years ago, perhaps even ten, Monroe would never have been able to sucker-punch him the way he did. Perhaps it really was time to give it all up, let others take on the burden.

But what then his sense of duty? There weren't many trackers around nowadays. Almost all Indians who could help, apart from those few Navajos and Yaquis fighting Government forces over in Arizona, were in reservations. Cole was virtually the last of a dying breed.

She came back, drying her hands on a towel. He sat up, waiting for another onslaught. Instead, he saw the softening around her eyes as she spoke. "I'm not going to tell you not to go, there would be no point. But I'm asking you, Cole – you look after yourself and don't do anything stupid or foolhardy. You hear me?"

"I hear you."

"You really are an old fool, Reuben Cole. There'll be no more of these escapades after this is done."

He nodded and held out his hands for her to help him to his feet.

He held her close and kissed her. "What would I do without you?"

"What would you do? You'd be lying in your damn grave, Reuben Cole, that's what you'd be doing!"

He smiled, knowing he couldn't disagree.

CHAPTER TWENTY-TWO

STEPPING up to the open double doors, Ryan Stone knocked tentatively before shouting out, "Anybody home?" Receiving no answer, he went inside anyway, taking off his hat and pausing to listen.

From somewhere he could make out the grunts and groans of someone moving things around. Heavy things by all accounts. It was the voice of a man, so he called again, "Mr Cartwright? It's Sheriff Stone, I've come to ask you a few things regarding the hotel."

He waited.

If it was Lewis Cartwright moving things, he clearly did not hear the Sheriff.

As far as Stone could tell, the voice seemed to be coming from underneath the floor. He peeped over the reception desk and frowned.

Spread across the top of the desk were a number of formal looking documents, embossed with stamps to prove their legality. Unable to suppress the urge, Stone picked one up and started to read.

The first thing that captured his attention was the name of the lawyer's office that had drawn up the document. Intrigued, he scanned through that and the other papers, some of which were statements made to the courts. Nancy Mumford's was there, which he found particularly interesting, as well as the legal document which transferred certain holdings to her grandchildren.

Certain holdings. He pondered on what that phrase might mean, but certainly there was enough information here for him to question Lewis Cartwright.

Drawing in a deep breath, he moved into the small saloon bar. Behind the counter, he saw the open hatch. From here, the sounds were louder.

"Mr Cartwright?"

Again, there was no reply, so he descended the steep stairs. There weren't many, but even so, after a few steps, the gloom of the cellar became oppressive.

A small, flickering torch in the far corner dribbled out a poor excuse for light. Bent over, on hands and knees, Lewis Cartwright was using a short spade to dig at the earth. He was muttering to himself as he worked. Next to him was a growing pile of soil.

Stone stood and watched, wondering what it was Cartwright was searching for. The story Mrs Jenkins relayed came to him, that niggling suspicion that all of this was to do with that mention of deeds. Deeds for what? Worth killing for all those years ago, and still now?

"Mr Cartwright?"

Squawking, Lewis span around, his eyes flashing white in the half-light. His face glistened with sweat, his breathing coming in short, sharp rasps. "Sheriff? What is it you want?"

"I can see you're busy, Mr Cartwright. I can come back."

"Eh?" He looked about him, quickly dusted off his trousers, and stood up. "No, no, I'm just fixing some pipes."

"Pipes?"

Cartwright grinned, but it was forced. False. Stone could clearly see the man's panic.

"Yes. Water pipes. I'm trying to fix the supply so it'll reach the upstairs rooms." Laughing, he came forward, took Stone by the elbow, and led him towards the stairs. "Now then, Sheriff, what is this all about?"

"Some questions, Mr Cartwright. About the murder."

Cartwright swayed backwards, Stone's words like slaps across his face. "The *murder*? I know nothing about it. The first I knew was after we'd gone to your office and—"

"No, no, Mr Cartwright, I'm talking about the murder that occurred here. The murder of Mr Mumford."

Cartwright's mouth gaped open as if in shock. Dragging his arm across his brow, he looked around him, reached for the torch, and motioned towards the stairs. "Let's discuss this upstairs, Mr Stone."

They both stomped up the stairs, the brightness of the saloon bar causing Stone to squint as he emerged from below.

Behind him, he heard Cartwright clinking glasses together. "Care for a drink, Sheriff?"

Stone turned to see Cartwright already pouring out two shots of whisky. "Don't mind if I do," he said, taking the proffered glass. He breathed in the smoky aroma and nodded appreciatively.

"Only the best," said Cartwright, downing his whisky in one. Smacking his lips, he raised his glass and studied it. "I'm not such a great drinker, but I do partake now and again." So saying, he poured himself a second shot. "So, Sheriff, what brings you here is the murder? The Mumford case, is that the one? I have to tell you, Sheriff, I don't know all that much."

"I thought the Reverend Peters told you about it?" Stone took a small sip of his drink, his eyes never leaving Cartwright.

The other man stopped, poised in the act of finishing his second glass. "Ah, so *that* was the one."

"Have there been others?"

"Others? What do you mean by that?"

"I mean the murder of Henry Jenkins."

Cartwright kept his eyes away from Stone's, preferring to focus them on his drink. "I wouldn't know."

"Really?" Stone carefully set the glass on the countertop. "I couldn't help noticing the papers you have left lying around, Mr Cartwright. The ones with Henry Jenkins' stamp on them? They detail an agreement made by Nancy Mumford, leaving certain trusts to her grandchildren."

"Ah." Cartwright smiled and downed his drink. Smacking his lips, he spoke in a solemn tone. "I'm afraid none of that has anything to do with me, Sheriff."

"Oh? Then who has it to do with?"

"Me, Sheriff."

Giving a slight start, Stone turned towards the sound of the voice. Sarah Cartwright stood in the doorway, her face blank of expression. She slowly moved forward.

"Mrs Cartwright," said Stone, unconsciously moving his hand to his hat to touch the brim. "I don't quite get your meaning."

"It's simple," said Cartwright, slipping beside Stone to join his wife. He was smiling, an expression made more powerful by the revolver he now held in his hand. "I'll ask you to very slowly throw your gun down, Sheriff. Easy does it, for your own sake."

Staring at the barrel of the gun, Stone knew he had little choice. With finger and thumb, he lifted his gun from its holster and dropped it to the floor.

Sarah dipped down and scooped the gun up.

"This is most inconvenient," said Cartwright. "It's a pity you arrived when you did. Another fifteen minutes or so, we would be gone."

"I don't understand," said Stone, looking from one to the other.

"It's quite simple," said Sarah. "I am Nancy Mumford's granddaughter. The deeds to the gold mine belong to me and my brother. We're here to collect."

"Goldmine?" Stone shook his head. "There ain't been any gold mined here for almost fifty years!"

"That's where you're wrong," said Cartwright. "Mumford found it, you see. Worked it for nearly five years. Dug out a mass of gold which he buried away for safe keeping. The mine he signed over to his wife. He was sick. Dying. He wanted her to have it to pass onto their children's children."

"And then she got herself involved with Silas Morgan, and the situation changed a little. But not so much that the claim was revoked. Our lawyer, Mr Jenkins, saw to that."

"But Jenkins is dead." Stone snapped his head around to Cartwright, lips drawn over his teeth, snarling, "You murdered him, didn't you?"

Cartwright's laughter rang out loud and brutal throughout the hotel. "Murdered Jenkins? Are you mad?"

"We didn't murder anyone," said Sarah quickly.

"Then who did?"

"You know full well – the men who forced their way into his home, to threaten him, demand he hand over the claim to the mine. The same men who assaulted Claudette Gower, abducting her to make her, or Jenkins, give up those deeds."

Stone's frown grew deeper. "Claudette Gower? What has she to do with any of this?"

"You really don't know anything, do you, Sheriff." Sarah shook her head sadly.

"Then maybe you should tell me, before I arrest you both and see you stand trial."

"You seem to forget it's us that have the drop on

you, Sheriff," said Cartwright, sneering. To add emphasis, he wiggled the gun in his hand.

"You wouldn't dare shoot an officer of the law," said Stone defiantly. "Now, tell me what this is all about before I arrest you!"

Now it was Sarah's turn to burst out with a loud guffaw. "Arrest us, for what?"

"Holding me up for a start! Hindering my investigation, withholding evidence. The list is long, Mrs Cartwright. You have a lot of explaining to do." He puffed out his chest. "Who was responsible for murdering Mr Jenkins?"

"Sebastian Monroe," said Sarah without a pause. Then, a slight smile. "My brother."

CHAPTER TWENTY-THREE

LEANING with his back against the outside wall, Peters closed his eyes, doing all he could to calm himself. He'd heard everything, the revelations hitting him hard. To think that these two newcomers were capable of such …

Slowly, he let out a long breath and allowed his eyes to settle on the Winchester. It would take all but a moment to burst in on them, shoot one of them – probably Cartwright – and save the Sheriff and wrap everything up into a neat parcel.

A moment.

It had taken him only moments to shoot down those boys. Innocent boys for all he knew. Their deaths changed him, their faces tormenting him through long, sleepless nights, forcing him to seek a new direction for his life. Turning his back on the Army, he joined a seminary college. A difficult time. So many questions about himself, his motivation, his faith. Faith. What was that, in the end? An acceptance that something beyond knowing watched over us, guided us, gave us the answers if we were willing to look? He didn't know. He thought he did, but not now. Seeing Jenkins lying there, the rage it caused, it made him realise he had never truly changed. He remained that same man, that killer. He always would be.

Checking the Winchester one last time, Peters took a breath, stepped away from the wall, and kicked his way through the main entrance to the hotel.

———

Cole cantered into town, moving easily past the saloon to the Sheriff's office. There he dismounted and tied the reins loosely to the hitching rail. Inside he found Matthias Thurst brewing coffee, and Amelie Gower sat behind Stone's desk, writing furiously.

Mrs Jenkins appeared to be napping in the corner. Perhaps for the best, thought Cole.

Amelie looked up, her face creasing into a frown. "Why, Mr Cole," she said. Her voice held no hint of welcome or relief, more one of thinly disguised distaste.

"Ah, Reuben," said Thurst, pouring out steaming coffee into tin cups, "care for some?"

"No thanks, Matthias. Hasn't Ryan returned yet?"

"Nope," said Matthias, handing a cup to Amelie, whose mouth turned down at the corners. She gave a brief, barely perceptible nod and took a sip.

"And where's the Reverend?"

"He went to see where Mr Stone was," replied Amelie, taking the opportunity to push the coffee away from her. She studied it in disgust as if it were an abhorrence.

"Hotel," put in Thurst, drinking his own coffee with relish.

"Well, we need to get going while there is still light." Cole turned to Amelie, who had recommenced writing. "What is that you're doing, if you don't mind me asking, ma'am?"

Pausing, head down, she appeared to be steadying

herself, searching for the right words to say. "It's a testimony, Mr Cole, if you must know."

"A testimony? What kind of testimony?"

"One for the Sheriff." Her head came up, her clear blue eyes piercing, glinting with that look of contempt Cole now recognised so easily. "A lawman, Mr Cole. Not a hired killer."

"Is that what you see me as, ma'am? A hired killer?"

"It's what you do isn't it? You hunt people down and execute them."

Behind Cole, Thurst whistled. "Ma'am, I don't think you fully know what you're saying when you accuse—"

"Excuse me," snapped Amelie Gower, "I know *precisely* what I'm saying." She set her unblinking gaze on Cole once more. "I've heard the stories. I know all about you, Mr Cole. When I have finished this," she prodded the paper with a stiff index finger, "Mr Stone can proceed with a lot more certainty. And by the way," she picked up her pen again, "I am a *Miss*."

Cole and Matthias shared a quick look.

"I'd appreciate that coffee now," said Cole, "if it's all right with you."

As Mathias went to reach for the coffee pot, the first gunshot rang out. He jumped, the tin cup in his hand falling to the floor with a loud clatter.

Amelie gave a cry of alarm.

Cole was already turning for the door when the second shot came.

It took only a moment for the Reverend Peters to assess the situation.

He saw Cartwright's open mouth, Stone's hands held out in supplication, and Sarah, turning, the gun in her hand.

Peter dropped to his knees, making himself as small

as possible. He put a bullet into Cartwright, throwing him backwards against the saloon bar counter. Cartwright cried out, grimacing, instinctively grasping for his back despite the bullet in his left shoulder. He fell, his revolver clattering to the ground.

Sarah's gun, the one snatched when Stone dropped it, barked once, but the bullet went hopelessly wild, her chosen target no longer there. Reacting with pure instinct, Stone rushed her from behind and wrestled with her, one arm across her throat, his other hand twisting the gun from her grip. She struggled, screaming insanely, a stream of obscenities issuing from her mouth. Stone held on, gritting his teeth. She was strong, far stronger than he expected, and she was wriggling free, turning, swinging her knee upwards.

Stone screeched high-pitched as her knee connected and released his hold.

"No," said Peters, climbing to his feet, the Winchester aiming. But could he be sure his aim was true? The two of them fought frantically, and if he fired, who would he hit?

Sarah's elbow snapped into Stone's face, sending him sprawling backwards. He fell on top of Cartwright who, bleeding profusely, still managed to bring his firearm to bear.

Peter hesitated.

In those few gaping, terrible seconds, everything flashed before him. Those faces, those boys dying because of him. He should have paused that day, considered his actions before emptying the Winchester into them. Innocent or guilty, they were young, their entire lives ahead of them. Peters had snuffed out their existence without a thought. He was determined not to make the same mistake again.

He stared deep into Cartwright's eyes and saw the man smile.

"Shoot him, Lewis! Shoot him!"

Peters heard the terrible, solid click of the hammer and knew his time had come.

"*Padre,*" came a voice, "*get out of the damned way!*"

Cole moved fast, shouldering the Reverend Peters with a powerful shunt just in time. Cartwright's bullet whizzed past and slapped into the double-door woodwork right behind where the Reverend had been standing. The Model 10 already in his hand, Cole fired twice, the first shot hitting Cartwright in the chest, driving him backwards, the second into his heart. He slumped across Stone, dead.

Screaming hysterically, Sarah Cartwright made a lunge for Stone's gun, but Cole was there first, kicking it out of reach. She rounded on him like a harpy, snarling, hands outstretched, fingers like claws preparing to strike. Without hesitation, Cole swung his fist into the side of her jaw, and it was over.

"I messed up," said Ryan Stone, head in hands, sitting on a barstool in the saloon some thirty or so minutes later.

"Don't be too hard on yourself," said Cole, sliding a full shot of whisky towards the hapless sheriff. "You weren't to know they would turn out that way."

"I should have waited for you. Every manual says never go into a situation alone. I ignored it, and look where it got me."

"Ryan, we learn by our mistakes. Darn it, if I were to count up how many times I've—"

"I could have died, Mr Cole. If it hadn't been for the Reverend, I almost certainly would be dead."

"Yeah," breathed Peters from the far end, rolling his

glass between the palms of his hands, "and if it hadn't have been for Cole here, I'd be dead too." He chuckled, raised his glass, and downed it in one.

"What's done is done," said Cole. "We now have to concentrate on the others."

"I'm not going with you," said Stone in a flat, depressed voice. "I'll stay here, take Sarah Cartwright's statement, if she's willing. If not, I can use Amelie Gower's and send a telegram to the circuit judge."

"I've yet to read what Miss Gower had to say."

"Put short, it lays out everything. We know Monroe is Sarah's brother, thanks to what she told us. It seems he met Claudette last year, and they became more than intimate. She told him she had the means for them both to run away, set up on their own in another place."

"Ryan, she's got to be at least twenty years his senior!"

Stone shrugged. "An attractive woman, but you're right. Clearly Monroe encouraged her, and she told him everything – her 'secret' so to speak. She and her sister had been contracted to clean up the hotel for the previous owner. It was while they were doing so that they came across copies of the deeds."

"She stole them?"

"No, she took them to Jenkins, who confirmed they were genuine. It's common for such documents to have several copies made. She kept them, told Monroe all about them. Then, to make things simpler, the previous owner went and died, the hotel was put up for sale, and the Cartwright's swooped."

"Thanks to Monroe's information about the deeds?"

Stone spread out his hands. "Poor Claudette didn't know anything about it. Monroe broke it off with her, and she went into a deep depression. He went to her to get the deeds, she refused, so he kidnapped her, hoping to put pressure on Jenkins. Her life for the deeds."

"And when that didn't happen, Jenkins got himself killed."

"Which leaves," put in Peters, "poor Claudette. I wonder if she's still alive."

"Let us hope so. You saw her, Cole, before Monroe slugged you."

"I saw a bundle lying on the ground. I couldn't tell if she was dead or not."

"Then we have to find out."

Nodding, Cole gave a long sigh. "Could be a U.S. Marshal will come across seeing as all of it is to do with past crimes. It'll get complicated."

"Not if you bring those others in."

Cole cleared his throat, shot a glance at Peters before lifting his glass towards the sheriff and saying, "Tell Maddie, won't you, Ryan. Tell her I'm off out on the range again, only this time I'm with the Padre." He finished his whisky. "I mean Reverend. No offence."

"None taken," said Peters, "but to be honest, I'm all done-in, Cole. As soon as we've brought those no-gooders in, I'll be sending out my own telegram, to the diocese in Denver. I'm quitting."

The others stopped and stared.

"It's a long story," he said, without further explanation. "I'll get the horses ready."

"There goes a man with a lot of problems resting on those big shoulders," said Stone as Reverend Peters plodded out of the saloon.

"I reckon he's had what you'd call a 'moral dilemma.'"

"What's that?"

Cole smirked. "I have no idea, just something Sterling used to say."

"You miss him, don't you, Mr Cole?"

"Every day."

Cole swung around and took a step towards the batwing doors.

"Mr Cole," said Stone quickly, "I sure hope you ain't gonna get yourself into another Monroe situation."

"Only situation I'll be getting into with Monroe is gonna be a mighty troublesome one," said Cole over his shoulder, then added: "For him."

CHAPTER TWENTY-FOUR

MONROE leaned closer, took Claudette's forearm in a vice-like grip and pulled her to him.

"What you really do have to understand, my darling, is that you have no choice in any of this. No choice at all."

Her fear was absolute, but even that could not prevent her from voicing her dissent. "I can't help you. What you're asking me to do ... I can't."

His eyes narrowed, "You're not listening to me," he hissed dangerously. "You have *no choice!*" His companions threw Monroe several inquisitive glances, but his fierce gaze prevented any of them from questioning him. He forced a smile, but there was strain in his face now. "It is time for you to follow my command. When you first came to me, you knew you had to do as you were told. I warned you what would happen if you didn't, that you would be asked to do things that you would find hard, even repulsive. You swore you would do as you were told, and there can be no going back from that. The consequences are total, for you. God will not forget the oath you made, under His name."

Tears welled up in her eyes. Clearly his grip caused her great pain, and all she could manage was a weak shake of the head. "I thought you loved me."

He barked out a laugh. "Love? *You*? You're old and all worn out, Claudette."

"I hate you," she said, tearing her head from those blazing eyes. "You used me, Sebastian. You thought you could control me, and you almost did, but then you left me. Why couldn't you just have stayed away?"

"I need those deeds. I need to know where the gold is buried."

"There is no gold, you oaf!"

He struck her without warning, knocking her backwards. She cowered on the ground, one hand against her mouth where the blood trickled from her cut lip.

"I killed Jenkins, who was as stubborn as you. You'll go back into town, find my sister, and together you'll get to the bottom of this. Jenkins' wife is an old witch, but she'll trust you. You'll convince her to hand over the deeds and then—"

"I'll not do anything to help you," she said, trying to sound brave.

Monroe laughed again. "Oh, yes, you will, or I'll go back into town and kill your sister. And I'll let you watch before I do the same for you."

"You're a monster."

"Indeed, I am, my little pretty one." His smile grew almost pleasant. "Old you may be, but you still is one damned attractive woman. Perhaps when this is all over, we could set up somewhere, you and me? What do you say?"

The only reply he received was a look of utter contempt.

The two men reined in their horses, pausing to lift canteens to dry lips and gulp down water. Peters adjusted himself in his saddle. "How do you manage to sit in one of these things for hours on end," he grimaced. "My backside feels as if it's perched on a bed of nails."

"Bed of nails? What's that?"

"Sore is what it is, Cole. I'm going to have to get down for a moment."

He did so, stretched out his back and rubbed his behind vigorously with both hands. "I can't feel it at all, save for the pain."

"I take it you don't ride a whole lot?"

"Not if I can help it," Peters shook his head. "You think we'll find them?"

"Yup," said the scout, pointing to the broken ground. "Signs are easy to follow. Perhaps too easy. I'm thinking they won't be expecting anyone to come after 'em. They left me out to die, as they did Ryan, so they is brim-full of confidence. My guess is they will be returning to the town soon to make another attempt to find the gold."

"Gold we now know doesn't exist."

"Yeah, but they don't know that."

"And Miss Claudette? What'll they do when they discover the truth? That all of this mayhem has been for nothing and that Sarah Cartwright is in jail, all her plans in shreds?"

Shrugging, Cole allowed his eyes to roam across the open expanse of the plain. "You know what they'll do. What *we* have to do is find 'em and bring 'em in."

Muttering to himself, Peters climbed onto the back of his horse again and twitched the reins. "Let's get to it." And they both set off once more, heads down, huddled up against the pulsing heat of the cruel, burning sun.

Cole spotted the tell-tale clouds of dust and knew what they were before he brought his telescope up to confirm it.

"It's them. Three men and a woman."

"Claudette?"

"I guess so," said Cole, snapping the telescope shut. "We need to take it easy on this, Reverend. At the first sign of trouble, they could well kill her."

"Then we shoot 'em stone dead!" He smacked the stock of his Winchester hanging from his saddle.

"You is awful keen on that, Reverend."

"I'm sick of it all, Cole. I want this done."

"When you said you was quitting the Church, have you a mind to become a bounty hunter, is that it?"

"I've had it with piety and forgiveness. It doesn't do any good."

"An eye for an eye, is that it?"

"Yes it is."

"I understand how you feel, Reverend. I understand a helluva lot, but we cannot sacrifice the woman. We have to be careful."

"How you propose we do that."

Cole motioned towards some broken ground, with sharp protruding rocks jutting upwards. "You wait there. You spook the horses with concentrated fire when they is close enough, and I will come in from the rear to rescue Claudette."

"You think you can do that, Cole? I mean, you aren't exactly a spring chicken anymore, are you."

Through gritted teeth, Cole snarled, "You just do what I say, Reverend, and leave everything else to me." He kicked his horse and set off on a sweeping ride way off to the right.

Peters moved his mount towards the rocks, taking his time, jaw set, eyes to the ground. He felt detached, the forces of fate bringing him to this moment. There was not a single thing he could do to prevent it. He was in Cuba once again, events dictating his actions, taking away his power of choice.

Although, this time, he had already made his choice.

Despite what Cole said, Peters was adamant. He refused to be a pawn in a massive game of chance. He'd seize the initiative, take the appropriate action and end this heinous tale of greed and murder.

CHAPTER TWENTY-FIVE

"**A**re you sure this is for the best?"

They were moving steadily across the plain, Monroe in the lead with Claudette Gower sitting astride a bedraggled old nag next to him.

With no answer forthcoming, Braddock pressed his companion. "Seb? Did you hear me?"

"I heard you."

"Then answer me! What we're doing, riding back to that town, I can't see as it is the right thing to do. They'll be waiting for us."

"Who?" Monroe eased his horse to a halt, allowing Braddock to move alongside. "Who is there to wait for us, eh? The Sheriff will be dead by now, that Cole is finished. There ain't no one else."

Hemmings cleared his throat as he pushed back his hat and wiped his brow with his sleeve. "The deputy?"

"That old tub of guts?" Monroe cackled and shot a look towards Claudette. "There ain't nobody else to worry about, is there, sweet thing?"

Claudette's icy glare gave him all the answers he needed.

Monroe took a few regular breaths and stared into the distance. "We'll hook up with Sarah and get the gold." He smiled. "Claudette has been forthcoming at last. So, by this evening, we will rich, boys. Rich."

Shaking his head, Braddock lowered his voice. "How you know she is telling the truth, Seb? What if we're riding into a trap?"

"She's telling me the truth because she knows I'll kill her and her sister if what she said is not so."

Something passed between Braddock and Hemmings. "All right, but we need to be careful. Even if that deputy is not much, he could gather together a bunch of townsfolk."

"Nah, I put the frighteners on them when Cole was looking for a posse. No one will dare stand against us."

"But that was before you killed that lawyer," put in Hemmings. "They'll be angry, Seb. They'll be looking to lynch us."

Laughing, Monroe flicked the reins and set off again at a gentle canter. "We'll burn the whole town, boys. Fear is the only weapon we'll need."

"You truly are a monster," said Claudette, body jerking forward as her horse, tethered to Monroe's, moved forward.

"Sure am," cackled Monroe, "but I reckon that's why you're so sweet on me."

From his vantage point far behind the group, Cole watched through his telescope, saw them discussing something, but could not make out their features or reactions. No matter, he sensed there was conflict, something that might work to his advantage. He had faith in the Reverend, knew the man could shoot and was convinced the ensuing confusion caused by his well-placed shots would ensure everything came out well in the end.

Blind faith in a man he hardly knew.

What else did he have?

Snapping the telescope shut, he let out a loud, long

sigh. This life, with its constant physical and mental struggle, was proving too much. The years were rolling by, and age was taking its toll and changing him. He remembered how Monroe had slinked up behind him so easily, and he shuddered at the memory. By rights, he should be dead. His luck, he knew, could only last out for so long. Perhaps this was it, the last call. The three men he hunted were hard, vicious, acting without conscience. Especially Monroe. For the first time, he could not predict the outcome. When Ryan Stone had saved him not so long ago, it struck him how fragile his hold on life was. Maddie brought him hope, love, a means to begin again despite the years. His answer was to set out again, on the trail to death. Those men, that swarm of murderous crows, picking at the carcasses, taking and doing as they pleased, they caused him to question his abilities, his desire to get the job done. At least this time, he had the Reverend, a man at odds with himself, but a man who tilted the odds in his favour. For one last time.

He mounted up, checked his Smith and Wesson, set his face against the dwindling, shadowy figures ahead, and moved on.

CHAPTER TWENTY-SIX

Peters watched their approach and felt the knot tightening in his gut.

Cole's orders had been precise – shoot to spook the horses. Cole knew, as indeed did he, that once the shooting started, Monroe and his gang would fight. To the death if need be. Spooking the horses might work, but only if Cole acted fast.

From where he sat, crouched behind a cluster of rocks and dried up scrub, there was no sign of the old scout.

Peters' pulse raced, filling up a throat already dry with anxiety. Unable to swallow, he reached for his canteen and took a long drink. The water hit the back of this throat as if it were scalding hot, and he coughed and spluttered, panicked in case any of Monroe's men heard him, and ducked down behind the boulder.

He waited, senses straining.

There appeared to be no reaction, and he chanced a look.

The first shot ricocheted from the top of the rocks, immediately accompanied by wild whooping as Monroe's men kicked their horses into action. The Reverend ducked down as Monroe fired off a second round, the red-hot lead smacking against the boulder inches from Peters' head.

"Damn it!" Peters blurted and tried to bring his Winchester up to at least give some semblance of a retort.

The whooping grew louder. They were close. In that desperate glance he managed to take, Peters saw Monroe wheeling away, taking Claudette with him. She was screaming, and he clubbed her across the side of the head with his pistol. Silenced, she tumbled from her saddle and hit the ground with a sickening, hollow thud.

Incensed, Peters pushed away all his uncertainties. Leaping to his feet, he took a bead on the first rider and shot him out of the saddle. He saw the look of disbelief crossing the man's face, mouth open in a silent scream as he pitched over, blood pumping from the wound in his chest.

Peters froze.

Locked in the moment, unable to tear his eyes away, he watched the man squirming on the ground, frantic fingers clawing at the wound, desperate to stop the flow of that thick, red blood.

So much blood.

He recalled Shepherd, body going into spasm, legs kicking in an insane attempt to escape, to flee from the certainty of his death.

And the blood, of course.

So much blood.

Barely conscious of his surroundings, the Reverend could not prevent the Winchester slipping from his grip. It clattered against the rocks, but he paid no heed. Time stopped. He was there, in that Cuban pueblo once again, Shepherd crying out, "Peters, Peters help me!"

But he could not help. He could do nothing, all of his strength gone.

Trapped and alone in an endless, black tunnel, its sides crushing him, squeezing, forever squeezing, he opened his mouth, battled to force out a scream, anything to help him return to the present, but it was useless.

"Peters!"

A bullet hit him in the shoulder, spinning him around, the scorching, instant pain bringing with it a fleeting, tentative awareness of his surroundings. Blinking, the figure of the gunman came into view, striding towards him, handgun held straight out, the grin splitting his sun-blackened face.

"Peters, get down!"

Those words did not come from the advancing gunman's mouth.

No, they came from somewhere beyond him. Somewhere far away. But he didn't care. He knew it was too late, and Peters closed his eyes and prepared himself to embrace this long hoped for moment of release.

Cole was dropping from his saddle before his horse came to a complete stop. The ground was hard underfoot, his running uncertain, ragged. A man past his prime, but a man filled with grim determination. Peters was out of his mind, standing out in the open. What was he doing?

He saw the first gunman falling from his horse, struck by Peters' first shot. Perhaps it was all going to work out fine. Perhaps Claudette could recover from that vicious blow from Monroe's gun. He didn't know. All he did know was what he saw.

Peters, now a statue, mouth opening and closing, lost in a nightmare world of indecision, possibly even fear. He saw him shot.

All of this, everything, so wrong, happening somewhere else in a distant place. Detached, disbelieving,

Cole shouted for the Reverend to get down. But the man didn't. He stood transfixed, and when the second bullet streaked past, he didn't flinch.

Cursing, Cole rushed on. He checked to his right. There was Monroe dismounting, sliding the Winchester from its scabbard. There was nothing anyone could do. The inevitable moment, the end of everything. Claudette unconscious, Peters about to die and Cole ...

Damn it, if only Sterling was here.

Cole fired his gun, the bullet slapping into the ground next to the gunman's foot. He spun around, fear mixing with the total shock of this new development.

"Sterling, where are you when I need you?"

The gunman's face changed, the eyes narrowing, the teeth clenched. Cole recognised it. The stone killer gaze.

Cole shot him three times, sending him jumping and jerking backwards, body perforated with tiny eruptions of gore.

Without pausing, Cole raced forward, feeling the tightness in his chest, his lungs bursting, all those years of inactivity, of sitting on the porch watching the world pass by. His muscles screamed, legs like lead, sweat rolling down into his eyes.

Eyes that locked in on those of Peters.

The Reverend's hands spread out, as if he were offering himself, surrendering to his fate. The tears sprang forth and tumbled down his cheeks. "I can't," he said. There was no more.

In those last, desperate strides, Cole wanted to charge into him, send him to the ground, to safety, but the distance seemed so great. Even so, he had to try. As he gathered himself for one, final effort, Monroe's Winchester rang out and Peters' head exploded like a ripe pumpkin, sending out a spray of pink mist to splatter against Cole's shirt front.

Keeling sideways, Peters fell like a great tree, and the silence engulfed them all.

Monroe cackled. This was easier than a turkey-shoot at the local fair. He worked the lever and brought it to his shoulder. "You're gonna die now, Cole," he breathed.

"A monster."

He snapped his head around.

It was Claudette, one side of her head swollen like a huge, purple, overripe piece of fruit. It oozed blood and one of her eyes was almost completely closed over. Despite this, and the obvious pain she was in, she grinned.

Monroe saw why and he understood.

From his horse she'd taken the knife. Its heavy blade glinted in the sun, her knuckles showing white in the tightness of her grip.

She lunged without warning. Monroe dodged and managed to divert the full force of the thrust. The razor-sharp edge sliced through his side, opening up his torso as if it were thin rice paper. He staggered backwards, and Claudette pressed forward, the knife arm coming up in preparation for the killing strike.

Like a drunkard, Cole staggered forward. There was no time to dwell on the poor Reverend because Claudette was in trouble. Serious trouble. Through scalding eyes, breathing laboured, Cole forced his body to eat up those last few paces.

Even then he realised he was too late.

Monroe, gasping from the initial knife attack, worked the Winchester and shot Claudette through the body. As she crumpled, he put another round into her. She floundered, arms outstretched, losing the grip on the knife. She wailed.

Cole roared.

Monroe turned, the wound in his side causing him to buckle. He tried to bring the Winchester to bear, but Cole got there first and emptied the Smith and Wesson into him. Two rounds. But it was enough.

Monroe fell, and Cole was on him, ripping the Winchester from his dying fingers, and clubbed him mercilessly with the stock, pounding him into oblivion.

He didn't stop, and there wasn't anyone left to tell him to.

CHAPTER TWENTY-SEVEN

I N the cool of the evening, Maddie slid closer to Cole on the porch swing they shared and held him close.

"I'm done," he said.

"You've said that before and every time you've—"

"*No*," he said emphatically, "this is it. No more." He stretched out his hands and they were shaking. "You see that? Never, in all the years have I experienced this. "

She pressed her face into his chest. "You mean I get to keep you here all to myself, every day?"

"Every minute," and he kissed the top of her head. "Out there, in the middle of all that killing, the thought of leaving you ... It was too much, Maddie. It's time to give it up, for good."

She breathed heavily and snuggled even closer. He could not see her smile, but he could feel it and he knew it was all good.

They sat like that for some considerable time until the sound of an approaching rider brought them out of their shared reverie. It was Stone and, as he drew closer, he pulled on the reins and came to a gentle halt. He watched them from a distance and smiled as he slipped down from the saddle. He moved closer, cleared his throat, and mounted the steps.

"Good day to you both."

"Howdy, sheriff," said Maddie. Cole simply looked.

"Mr Cole, I'm sorry to bother you, but it's that marshal I spoke to you about. He's in town right now, doing the investigating, and he says—"

"Ryan, I couldn't give two hoots what some marshal says or doesn't say. I'm finished with it."

"Yeah, yeah, I know that, Mr Cole, but ..." He chewed at his bottom lips as he moved from one foot to the next.

"What is it, Ryan?" asked Maddie, her voice soft and silken in that tense, over-wrought atmosphere. "Just tell it."

"Well, Miss Maddie, he says whoever tried to stop the killing of Reverend Peters and Claudette Gower deserves a medal. He's overlooking a lot of it as those dead pieces of rat-filth were wanted right across Texas for all sorts of heinous things. He said he'd write up his report to show they were lawfully killed."

"And Mrs Cartwright?"

"She's gonna face trial. Poor Miss Amelie, she is in an awful way, crying all the while. The whole thing is ... pardon my language, Miss Maddie, but the whole damned thing was all for nothing. There never was no gold. It was all a lie cobbled together to secure a mortgage for the original purchase of the hotel. Everyone concerned, they all died for nothin'!"

"That's sad," said Maddie, squeezing Cole's hand. "But this land is full of sadness. All we can do is try our best to live with it."

Two days later, Cole returned from his usual early-morning ride to check the stock. He took his horse to the rear of the house, unsaddled her, and made his way back to the house. He stopped when he saw the little rig waiting outside and frowned.

Instinctively, his hand dropped to where his gun would wait. But not any longer. Unarmed, he sighed, chided himself and felt a little silly. Killers don't drive up in full daylight, nor did they drive small buggies.

At least, he hoped they didn't.

"Reuben!" shouted Maddie as Cole came through the door, knocking off the dust with his hat. She came towards him, arms wide open.

"This is Mr Casper from New York City." Sweeping her arm wide, she turned to reveal a small, dapper looking man sitting with his Derby hat on his knees, smiling awkwardly. He put down his coffee cup and stood up. "Mr Casper has a proposition for you, Reuben."

Frowning, Cole studied the little man's reddening face.

"I'm so very pleased to meet you," said Casper, standing up and coming forward. He moved tentatively, a little afraid. The hand he held out shook slightly.

Taking the hand, Cole noted how weak the man's grip was, the manicured fingernails, the softness of the flesh. This was a man who had rarely left the confines of his office. "If this is anything to do with banks or money, then I—"

"Oh no, not banking!"

"Reuben," put in Maddie, "Mr Casper writes for the *Harper's Weekly*. They publish tales about the Old West."

"Perhaps you've heard of us?"

Shrugging, Cole settled himself into his armchair and beckoned for Casper to sit. The little man's smile remained frozen on his lips. "I don't get much chance to read, Mr Casper."

"We have a loyal readership, Mr Cole, who are hungry for *factual* stories. Not Dime Novels, but the real thing."

Maddie busied herself with crossing over to the drinks cabinet in the corner. She spoke with her back to

Cole. "Reuben, Mr Casper is interested in hearing your stories, about what you did. You and Sterling."

Cole tilted his head. "What we did?"

"Yes," said Casper, leaning forward, eyes brim-full with enthusiasm. "There is a huge market for such stories, Mr Cole. As the West is now so much tamer, people are interested in discovering what it used to be like."

"Mr Casper, I just recently came back from a fire-fight which was anything but tame."

"That's just it, Reuben," said Maddie, moving up close to him with a full glass of whisky in her hand. "Mr Casper wants all of that, for his magazine. Monthly stories about the Old West. And Reuben," she dropped her voice, "he's gonna pay might handsomely."

Not convinced, Cole took the whisky and considered it for some moments. "To be honest, I'm not sure I want to relive all of that, Mr Casper."

"Oh, Reuben," snapped Maddie. "What else you gonna do, knocking your head against the walls in this place?"

"I have the stock, I have fences to fix, and—"

"Oh tosh, Reuben! It'll liven up your days. You can be out on the range again, with Sterling and the others without ever leaving the confines of this home. With the money we make, we can start to live real comfortable like."

"We already do."

"I want a new dress, Reuben, I want to go into town in a new buggy, to meet my old friends, take lunch ... Why, we could even hire a cook, a maid like Marta who looked after the house when your dear old pa was alive."

Cole drank his whisky, savouring the taste. Slowly, his eyes closed. Marta ...

"What would it entail?" he asked in a low, almost bored voice.

"Why, Mr Cole," said Casper, his voice rising a

couple of decibels, "we can write up a contract right now. Payments would be wired to from—"

"No, I mean what do *I* need to do, Mr Casper, about these stories?"

Cole's eyes snapped open and Casper, taken aback a little, spread out his hands. "Nothing at all, Mr Cole. You relay the tales to me, and I write them up. They will be published on a regular basis every three months or so."

"Mr Casper explained he would come here every few weeks, and you tell him what happened," explained Maddie, almost as if she were talking to a child. "It won't take no time at all, will it, Mr Casper?"

"None at all."

"Mr Casper will take the notes then return to New York and prepare them for publication. You'll be famous, Reuben."

"He Who Comes," said Casper.

Cole arched a single eyebrow. "You told him that, Maddie?"

"I did. It's what the Indians called you. I reckon some of the older ones still do."

"It's a great moniker, Mr Cole," said Casper.

"A great what?"

"Reuben," Maddie got down next to him, reached out and held his knee. "Reuben, think of it. The romance of the West. You and Sterling riding out across the plains, adventures, excitement."

"Romance?"

"It doesn't just mean kissing and stuff. It'll be like Robin Hood. You know him, don't you, Reuben."

Cole sat back, face turned to the ceiling, pondering a myriad of reasons why he should turn down the offer. There was no denying the money would be welcome. Times were hard: there was grain to buy, farriers to hire. It all cost. He sighed, surrendering. "When?"

"We can set to work within the next few days, Mr

Cole," said Casper, unable to keep the elation from his voice. "I promise you this will be a mutually beneficial arrangement. We have over a million readers, Mr Cole."

"Think of it, Reuben."

His head came down, and he looked into Maddie's beautiful face. "We could do with the money."

"Yes, we could."

"And if it ain't gonna be too taxing ..."

"It won't be," urged Casper.

Cole's smile broadened. "Then why not. It'll be good to revisit the old days, I guess. Without the danger of being shot, of course."

"Yes," said Maddie, grasping his hand and squeezing it. "Without the danger of any kind."

"All right then," and he turned to Casper. For the first time in many weeks, he smiled. "Where do I sign?"

Dear reader,

We hope you enjoyed reading *Murdered By Crows*. Please take a moment to leave a review, even if it's a short one. Your opinion is important to us.

Discover more books by Stuart G. Yates at

https://www.nextchapter.pub/authors/stuart-g-yates

Want to know when one of our books is free or discounted? Join the newsletter at

http://eepurl.com/bqqB3H

Best regards,

Stuart G. Yates and the Next Chapter Team

Murdered By Crows
ISBN: 978-4-86745-535-7

Published by
Next Chapter
1-60-20 Minami-Otsuka
170-0005 Toshima-Ku, Tokyo
+818035793528

7th April 2021